LEGEND

By Clemence Dane

—

NOVELS

REGIMENT OF WOMEN
FIRST THE BLADE
WANDERING STARS
THE BABYONS
BROOME STAGES
THE MOON IS FEMININE
THE ARROGANT HISTORY OF WHITE BEN
HE BRINGS GREAT NEWS

With Helen Simpson

ENTER SIR JOHN
PRINTER'S DEVIL
RE-ENTER SIR JOHN

OMNIBUS COLLECTION

RECAPTURE

VOLUME OF SHORT STORIES

FATE CRIES OUT

PLAYS

A BILL OF DIVORCEMENT
WILL SHAKESPEARE
THE WAY THINGS HAPPEN
NABOTH'S VINEYARD
GRANITE
MARINERS
WILD DECEMBERS
MOONLIGHT IS SILVER
COUSIN MURIEL
HEROD AND MARIAMNE
THE LION AND THE UNICORN

With Richard Addinsell

ADAM'S OPERA
COME OF AGE
ENGLAND'S DARLING
THE SAVIOURS

A POEM

TRAFALGAR DAY, 1940

ESSAYS

THE WOMAN'S SIDE
TRADITION AND HUGH WALPOLE

ANTHOLOGIES

A HUNDRED ENCHANTED TALES
THE SHELTER BOOK
THE NELSON TOUCH

LEGEND

BY

CLEMENCE DANE

GREENWOOD PRESS, PUBLISHERS
WESTPORT, CONNECTICUT

Library of Congress Cataloging in Publication Data

Ashton, Winifred.
  Legend.

    Reprint of the ed. first published in 1919 by
W. Heineman, London.
    I. Title.
PZ3.A8286Le 1978 [PR6001.S5] 823'.9'12   78-17053
ISBN 0-313-20572-8

.BEETHOVEN, Op. 57.

First published November 1919

Reprinted with the permission of Miss Olwen Bowen Davies

Reprinted in 1978 by Greenwood Press, Inc.
51 Riverside Avenue, Westport, CT. 06880

Printed in the United States of America

10 9 8 7 6 5 4 3 2 1

LEGEND

Messrs. Mitchell and Bent will shortly issue ' The Life of Madala Grey ' by Anita Serle: a critical biography based largely on private correspondence and intimate personal knowledge.

That was in *The Times* a fortnight ago. And now the reviews are beginning—

The Cult of Madala Grey. . .

The Problem of Madala Grey. . .

The Secret of Madala Grey. . .

I wish they wouldn't. Oh, I *wish* they wouldn't.

No admirer of the late Madala Grey's arresting art can fail to be absorbed by these intimate and unexpected revelations . . .

Delicately, unerringly, Miss Serle traces to its source the inspiration of that remarkable writer. . .

And—this will please Anita most of all—

We ourselves have never joined in the chorus of praise that, a decade ago, greeted the appearance of ' Eden Walls ' and its successors, and in our opinion Miss Serle, in her biographical enthusiasm, uses the word genius a little too often and too easily. Madala Grey has yet to be tried by that subtlest of literary critics, the Man with the Scythe. But whether or not we agree with Miss Serle's estimate of her heroine, there can be no two questions as to the literary value of the ' Life ' itself. It definitely places Miss Serle

LEGEND

*among the Boswells, and as we close its fascinating
pages we find ourselves wondering whether our grand-
children will remember Miss Serle as the biographer
of Madala Grey, or Madala Grey as the subject matter
merely, of a chronicle that has become a classic.*

That is to say—*La reine est morte. Vive la reine!*
Anita will certainly be pleased. Well, I suppose
she's got what she wants, what she's always wanted.
She isn't a woman to change. The new portrait in
the *Bookman* might have been taken when I knew
her : the mouth's a trifle harder, the hair a trifle
greyer; but no real change. But it amuses me
that there should be her portrait in all the papers,
and none of Madala Grey; not even in the *Life*
itself. I can hear Anita's regretful explanations
in her soft, convincing voice. She will make a
useful little paragraph out of it—

*Miss Serle, whose ' Life of Madala Grey ' is causing
no small stir in literary circles, tells us that the brilliant
novelist had so great a dislike of being photographed
that there is no record of her features in existence.
An odd foible in one who, in our own recollection,
was not only a popular writer but a strikingly beautiful
woman.*

And yet, from her heavy, solitary frame (we have
no other pictures in our den) that ' beautiful woman,'
with her flowered scarf and her handful of cowslips,
is looking down at this moment at me—at me, and
the press cuttings, and *The Times*, and Anita's
hateful book. And she says, unmistakeably—

2

' Does it matter ?   What does it matter ? ' laughing a little as she says it.

Then I laugh too, because Anita knows all about the portrait.

After all, does it matter ?   Does it matter what Anita says and does and writes ?   And why should I of all people grudge Anita her success ?   Honestly, I don't.   And I don't doubt that the book is well written : not that I shall read it.   There's no need : I know exactly what she will have written : I know how convincing it will be.   But it won't be true. It won't be Madala Grey.

Of course Anita would say—' My dear Jenny, what do you know about it ?   You never even met her.   You heard us, her friends, her intimates, talking about her for—how long?   An hour ? Two hours ?   And on the strength of that—that eaves-dropping five years ago ' (I can hear the nip in her voice still) ' you are so amusing as to challenge my personal knowledge of my dearest friend. Possibly you contemplate writing the story of Madala Grey yourself?   If so, pray send me a copy.'   And then the swish of her skirt.   She always wore trains in those days, and she always glided away before one could answer.

But I could answer.   I remember that evening so well.   I don't believe I've forgotten a word or a movement, and if I could only write it down, those two hours would tell, as Anita's book never will, the story of Madala Grey.

3

LEGEND

I ought to be able to write; because Anita is my mother's cousin; though I never saw her till I was eighteen.

Mother died when I was eighteen.

If she had not been ill so long it would have been harder. As it was—but there's no use in writing down that black time. Afterwards I didn't know what to do. The pension had stopped, of course. I'd managed to teach myself typing, though Mother couldn't be left much; but I didn't know shorthand, and I couldn't get work, and my money was dwindling, and I was getting scared. I was ready to worship Anita when her letter came. She was sorry about Mother and she wanted a secretary. If I could type I could come.

I remember how excited I was. I'd always lived in such a tiny place and we couldn't afford Mudie's. To go to London, and meet interesting people, and live with a real writer, seemed too good to be true. And it helped that Anita and her mother were relations. Mother used to stay with Great-aunt Serle when she was little. Somehow that made things easier to me when I was missing Mother more than usual.

In the end, after all those expectations, I was only three weeks with Anita. They were a queer three weeks. I was afraid of her. She was one of those people who make you feel guilty. But she was kind to me. I typed most of the day, for she was a fluent worker and never spared either of us; but

4

she took me to the theatre once, and I used to pour out when interesting people came to tea. In the first fortnight I met nine novelists and a poet; but I never found out who they were, because they all called each other by their Christian names and you couldn't ask Anita questions. She had such a way of asking you why you asked. She used to glide about the room in a cloud of chiffon and cigarette smoke—she had half-shut pale eyes just the colour of the smoke—and pour out a stream of beautiful English in a pure cool voice; but if they interrupted her she used to stiffen and stop dead and in a minute she had glided away and begun to talk to someone else. Old Mrs. Serle used to sit in a corner and knit. She never dropped a stitch; but she always had her eyes on Anita. She was different from the rest of my people. She had an accent, not cockney exactly, but odd. She had had a hard life, I believe. Mother said of her once that her courage made up for everything. But she never told me what the everything was. Great-aunt's memory was shaky. One day she would scarcely know you, and another day she would be sensible and kind, very kind. She liked parties. People used to come and talk to her because she made them laugh; but every now and then, when Anita was being brilliant about something, she would put up her long gnarled finger and say—'Hush! Listen to my daughter!' and her eyes would twinkle. But I never knew if she were proud of her or not.

5

LEGEND

Everybody said that Anita was brilliant. She could take a book to pieces so that you saw every good bit and every bad bit separated away into little compartments. But she spoiled things for you, books and people, at least she did for me. She sneered. She said of the Baxter girl once, for instance—'She's really too tactful. If you go to tea with her you are sure to be introduced to your oldest friend.' And again—'She always likes the right people for the wrong reasons.'

Of course one knows what she meant, but I liked the Baxter girl all the same. Beryl Baxter—but everyone called her the Baxter girl. She was kind to me because I was Anita's cousin, and she used to talk to me when Anita wasn't in the mood for her. She asked me to call her 'Beryl' almost at once. Anita used to be awfully rude to her sometimes, and then again she would have her to supper and spend an evening going through her MSS. and I could tell that she was giving her valuable help. The Baxter girl used to listen and agree so eagerly and take it away to re-write. I thought she was dreadfully grateful. I hated to hear her. And when she was gone Anita would lean back in her chair with a dead look on her face and say—

"God help her readers! Jenny, open the window. That girl reeks of patchouli." And then —"Why do I waste my time?"

And Great-aunt Serle in her corner would chuckle and poke and mutter, but not loud—

6

LEGEND

" Why does she waste her time?   Listen to my daughter ! "

The next time the Baxter girl came Anita would hardly speak to her.

The Baxter girl seemed to take it as a matter of course.   But once she said to me, with a look on her face as if she were defending herself—

" Ah—but you don't write. You're not keen. You don't know what it means to be in the set."

" But such heaps of people come to see Anita," I said, " people she hardly knows."

" They're only the fringes," said the Baxter girl complacently. " They're not in the Grey set. They don't come to the Nights. At least, only a few. Jasper Flood, of course—you've met him, haven't you?—and Lila Howe—*Masquerade*, you know, and *Sir Fortinbras*." The Baxter girl always ticketed everyone she mentioned. " And the Whitneys. She used to stay with the Whitneys. And Roy Huth. And of course Kent Rehan."

" Kent Rehan ? "

" *The* Kent Rehan," said the Baxter girl.

Then I remembered. The vicar's wife always sent Mother the Academy catalogue after she had been up to town. I used to cut out the pictures I liked, and I liked Kent Rehan's. They had wind blowing through them, and sunshine, and jolly blobs that I knew must be raw colour, and always the same woman. But you could never see her face, only a cheek curve or a shoulder line. They were

7

in the catalogue every year, and so I told the Baxter girl. She laughed.

"Yes, he's always on the line. Anita says that's the worst she knows of him. And of course the veiled lady——" she laughed again, knowingly, "But there is one full face, I believe. *The Spring Song* he calls it. But it's never been shown. Anita's seen it. She told me. He keeps it locked away in his studio. They say he's in love with her."

"With whom?"

"Madala Grey, of course."

I said—

"Who is Madala Grey?"

The Baxter girl had sunk into the cushions until she was prone. I had been wondering with the bit of mind that wasn't listening what the people at home would have said to her, with her cobweb stockings (it was November) and her coloured combs and her sprawl. It was a relief to see her sit up suddenly.

"'Who's Madala Grey!'" Her mouth stayed open after she'd finished the sentence.

"Yes," I said. "Who is she?"

"You mean to say you've never heard of Madala Grey? You've never read *Eden Walls?* Is there anyone in England who hasn't read *Eden Walls?*"

"Heaps," I said. She annoyed me. She—they—they all thought me a fool at Anita's.

The Baxter girl sighed luxuriously.

"My word, I envy you! I wish I was reading

8

Eden Walls for the first time—or *Ploughed Fields.*
I don't care so much about *The Resting-place.*"
She laughed. " At least—one's not supposed to
care about *The Resting-place,* you know. It's as
much as one's life's worth—one's literary life."

" What's wrong with it ? "

" Sentimental. Anita says so. She says she
doesn't know what happened to her over *The
Resting-place.*"

" I like the title," I said.

" Yes, so do I. And I love the opening where——
Oh, but you haven't read it. And you're Anita's
cousin ! What a comedy ! Just like Anita though,
not to speak of her."

" Why ? Doesn't Anita like her ? "

The Baxter girl was flat on the cushions again.
She looked at me with those furtive eyes that
always so strangely qualified her garrulity.

" Are you shrewd ? Or was that chance ? "

" What ? "

" ' Doesn't Anita like her ? ' "

" Doesn't she then ? "

" Ah, now you're asking ! Officially, very much.
Too much, *I* should say. And too much is just the
same as the other thing, I think. Would you like
Anita for your bosom friend ? "

Naturally I said—

" Anita's been very kind to me." Anita's my
cousin, after all. I didn't like the Baxter girl's tone.

" Oh, she's been kind to me." The Baxter girl

caught me up quickly. She was like a sensitive plant for all her crudity. " Oh, I admire Anita. She's the finest judge of style in England. Jasper Flood says so. You mustn't think I say a word against Anita. Very kind to me she's been." Then, innocently, but her eyes were flickering again —" She was kind to Madala too, till——"

" Well ? " I demanded

" Till Madala was kind to her. Madala's one of those big people. She'll never forget what she owes Anita—what Anita told her she owed her. After she made her own name, she made Anita's. Anita, being Anita, doesn't forget that."

" How d'you mean—made Anita's name ? "

" Well, look at the people who come here—the people who count. What do you think the draw was ? Anita ? Oh yes, *now*. But they came first for Madala. Oh, those early days when *Eden Walls* was just out ! Of course Anita had sense for ten. She ran Madala for all she was worth."

" Then you do like Madala Grey ? "

" I ? " The Baxter girl looked at me oddly. " She read my book. She wrote to me. That's why Anita took me up. She let me come to the Nights. She started them, you know. Somebody reads a story or a poem, and then it's talk till the milkman comes. Good times ! But now Madala's married she doesn't come often. Anita carries on like grim death, of course. But it's not the same. Last month it was dreary."

10

LEGEND

" Is it every month ? "

" Yes. It's tomorrow again. Tomorrow's Sunday, isn't it ? It'll amuse you. You'll come, of course, as you're in the house."

" Will she ? Herself ? " I found myself reproducing the Baxter girl's eagerness.

" Not now." The common voice had deepened queerly. " She's very ill." She hesitated. " That's why I came today. I thought Anita might have heard. Not my business, of course, but——" She made an awkward, violent gesture with her hands. " Oh, a genius oughtn't to marry. It's wicked waste. Well, so long ! See you tomorrow night ! "

She left me abruptly.

I found myself marking time, as it were, all through that morrow, as if the evening were of great importance. The Baxter girl was always unsettling, or it may have been Anita's restlessness that affected me. Anita was on edge. She was writing, writing, all the morning. She was at her desk when I came down. There was a mass of packets and papers in front of her and an empty coffee cup. I believe she had been writing all night. She had that white look round her eyes. But she didn't need any typing done. Early in the afternoon she went out and at once Great-aunt, in her corner, put down her knitting with a little catch of her breath. But she didn't talk : she sat watching the door. I had been half the day at the window, fascinated by the

11

fog. I'd never seen a London fog before. I found
myself writing a letter in my head to Mother about
it, about the way it would change from black to
yellow and then clear off to let in daylight and
sparrow-talk and the tramp-tramp of feet, and then
back again to silence, and the sun like a ball that you
could reach up to with your hand and hold. I was
deep in my description—and then, of a sudden, I
remembered that she wasn't there to write to any
more. It was so hard to remember always that she
was dead. I got up quickly and went to Anita's
shelves for a book. Great-aunt hadn't noticed
anything. She was still watching the door.

The little back room that opened on to the stair-
case was lined to the ceiling with books, all so tidy
and alphabetical. Anita lived for books, but I
used to wonder why. She didn't love them. Her
books never opened friendlily at special places, and
they hadn't the proper smell. I ran my finger along
the ' G's ' and pulled out *Eden Walls*.

I began in the middle of course. One always
falls into the middle of a real person's life, and a
book *is* a person. There's always time to find out
their beginning afterwards when you've decided to
be friends. It isn't always worth while. But it
was with *Eden Walls*. I liked the voice in which
the story was being told. Soon I began to feel
happier. Then I began to feel excited. It said
things I'd always thought, you know. It was
extraordinary that it knew how I felt about things.

LEGEND

There's a bit where the heroine comes to town and the streets scare her, because they go on, and on, and on, always in straight lines, like a corridor in a dream. Now how did she know of that dream? I turned back to the first page and began to read steadily.

When Anita's voice jerked me back to real life it was nearly dark. She was speaking to Great-aunt as she took off her wraps—

"The fog's confusing. I had to take a taxi to the tube. A trunk call is an endless business."

"Well?" said Great-aunt.

"Nothing fresh."

"Did *he* answer?"

Anita nodded.

"Was he——? Is she——? Did you ask——? What did he tell you, Anita?"

Anita stabbed at her hat with her long pins. She was flushing.

"The usual details. He spares you nothing. Have you had tea, Mother?" She rang the bell.

Great-aunt beat her hand on the arm of her chair in a feeble, restless way. When I brought her tea she said to me in her confidential whisper—

"Give it to my daughter. She's tired. She'll tell us when she's not so tired."

She settled herself again to watch; but she watched Anita, not the door.

And in a few minutes Anita did say, as the Baxter girl had said—

13

LEGEND

"She's very ill." And then—" I always told you we ought to have a telephone. I can't be running out all the evening."

"Do they come tonight?" said Great-aunt Serle. Anita answered her coldly—

"They do. Why not?"

Great-aunt tittered.

"Why not? Why not? Listen, little Jenny!"

Anita, as usual, was quite patient.

"Mother, you mustn't excite yourself. Jenny, give Mother some more tea. What good would it do Madala to upset my arrangements? Besides, Kent will have the latest news. I think you may trust him." She gave that little laugh that was Great-aunt's titter grown musical. Then she turned to me.

"By the way, Jenny, I expect friends tonight. You needn't change, as you're in mourning. You'll see to the coffee, please. We'll have the door open and the coffee in the little room. You might do it now while I dress."

The big drawing-room was divided from the little outer room by a curtained door. It was closed in the day-time for cosiness' sake, but when it was flung back the room was a splendid one. The small room held the books and a chair or two, and a chesterfield facing the door that opened on to the passage and the narrow twisting stairs. They were so dark that Anita kept a candle and matches in the hall: but one seldom troubled to light it. It

14

was quicker to fumble one's way. Anita used to long for electric light; but she would not install it. Anita had good taste. The house was old, and old-fashioned it should stay.

I fastened back the door and re-arranged the furniture, and was sitting down to *Eden Walls* again when Great-aunt beckoned me.

" Go and dress, my dear ! "

" But Anita said——" I began.

She held me by the wrist, all nods and smiles and hoarse whispers.

" The pretty dress—to show a pretty throat—isn't there a pretty dress somewhere? I know! Put it on. Put it on. What a white throat! I've a necklace somewhere—but then Anita would know. Mustn't tell Anita ! "

She pulled me down to her with fumbling, shaky hands.

" Tell me, Jenny, where's my daughter? "

" Upstairs, Auntie."

" Tell me, Jenny — any news? Any news, Jenny ? "

I didn't know what to say to her. I was afraid of hurting her. She was so shaking and pitiful.

" Is it about Miss Grey, Auntie ? "

" Carey, Jenny—Carey. Mrs. John Carey. Good name. Good man. But Anita don't like him. Anita won't tell me. You tell me, Jenny ! "

" Auntie, it's all right. It's all right. She'll tell you, of course, when she hears again." And I

soothed her as well as I could, till she let me loosen
her hand from my wrist, and kiss her, and start her
at her knitting again, so that I could finish making
ready the room.   But as I went to wash my hands
she called to me once more.

" Yes, Auntie ? "

" Put it on, Jenny.   Don't ask my daughter.   Put
it on."

She was a queer old woman.   She made me want
to cry sometimes.   She was so frightened always,
and yet so game.

But I went upstairs after supper and put on the
frock she liked.   Black, of course, but with Mother's
lace fichu I liked myself in it too.   I did my hair
high.   I don't know why I took so much trouble
except that I wanted to cheer myself up.   It had
been a depressing day in spite of *Eden Walls*.   I
looked forward to the stir of visitors.   And then I
was curious to see Kent Rehan.

When I came down the Baxter girl was already
there, standing all by herself at the fire.   She was
strikingly dressed;   but she looked stranded.   I
wondered if Anita had been snubbing her.

Anita was shaking hands with Mr. Flood and with
a lady whom I had not seen before.   She was
blonde, with greenish-golden hair and round eyes,
very black eyes that had no lights in them, not even
when she smiled.   She often smiled.   She had a
drawling voice and hardly spoke at all, except to
Mr. Flood.   If he talked to anyone else or walked

away from her, she would watch him fo a minute, and then say—'Jasper' with a sort of purr, not troubling to raise her voice. But he always heard and came. She wore a wonderful Chinese sha vl, white, with gold dragons worked on it, and whenever she moved it set the dragons crawling. She was powdered and red-lipped like a clown, and I didn't really like her, but nevertheless there was something about her that was queerly attractive. When she smiled at me because I gave her coffee, I felt quite elated. But I didn't like her. Mr. Flood called her ' Blanche.' I never heard her other name.

Anita seemed very pleased to see them. I caught scraps.

" Am so glad—one's friends about one—such a strain waiting for news. I phoned this afternoon. No, the usual phrases. Anxious, of course, but I should certainly have heard if—— Good of you to come ! No chance of the Whitneys, I'm afraid—too much fog. And what are you reading to us ? "

The Baxter girl, as I greeted her, stripped and re-dressed me with one swift look.

" My dear, it suits you ! I wish I could look Victorian. But I'm vile in black. Have you seen Lila ? I met her on the step. They've turned down *Sir Fortinbras* in America. Isn't it rotten luck ? Anita said they would. Anita's always right. Any more news of Madala ? "

Anita overheard her. She was suddenly gracious to the Baxter girl.

"You may be sure I should always let you know at once. And what is this I hear about Lila? Poor Lila! It's the last chapter, I'm afraid. I advised her from the beginning that the American public will not tolerate—but dear Lila is a law unto herself." And then, as Miss Howe came in—"Lila, my dear! How good of you to venture! A night like this makes me wonder why I continue in London. Madala has urged me to move out ever since—— No. No news. But Jasper's been energetic——" She circled mazily about them while I brought the coffee.

"Kent coming?" said Mr. Flood, fumbling with his papers.

Anita shrugged her shoulders.

"Who can account for Kent? It may dawn on him that he's due here—and again, it may not. It depends as usual, I suppose, on the new picture."

"Oh yes, there's a new one," recollected the Baxter girl carefully.

"There must be! He was literally flocculent yesterday." Miss Howe chuckled. "That can only mean one of two things. Art or——"

"—the lady! Who can doubt? Well, if Carey doesn't object to his brotherly love continuing, I'm sure I don't. But I wish it need not involve his missing his appointments." Mr. Flood eyed his typescript impatiently.

Anita was instantly all tact.

" Oh, we won't wait. Certainly not. Pull in to the fire. Now, Jasper ! "

But Miss Howe, as she swirled into Anita's special chair, her skirts overflowing either arm, abolished Mr. Flood and his typescript with a movement of her soft dimply hands.

" Oh, I'm not in the mood even for Jasper's efforts. I want to let myself go. I want to damn publishers—and husbands ! Damn them ! Damn them ! There ! Am I shocking you, Miss Summer ? " She smiled at me over their heads. She was always polite to me. I liked her. She was like a fat, pink pæony.

" Well, if you take my advice——" began Anita.

" My darling, I love you, but I don't want your advice. I only want one person's advice—ever— and she has got married and is doing her duty in that state of life—— Hence I say—Damn husbands ! I tell you I want Madala to soothe me, and storm at the injustice of publishers for me, and then—no, not give me a brilliant idea for the last chapter, but make me tell her one, and then applaud me for it. *You* know, Anita ! " She dug at her openly.

I caught a movement in Great-aunt's corner.

" Coffee, Auntie ? "

She gave me a goblin glance.

" My daughter ! " She had an air of introducing her triumphantly. " Listen ' She don't like fat women."

19

LEGEND

We listened. Anita's voice was mellow with cordiality.

" Yes indeed. Madala has often said to me that she thought you well worth encouraging."

Miss Howe laughed jollily.

" I admire your articles, Nita. I wilt when you review me. But you'll never write novels, darling. You've not the ear. Madala may have said that, but she didn't say it in that way."

" She certainly said it."

" Some day I'll ask her."

" Some day ! Oh, some day ! " The Baxter girl was staring at the fire. " Shall we ever get her back ? "

" In a year ! Let us give her a year ! " Mr. Flood looked up at the lady beside him with a thin smile. I couldn't bear him. He sat on the floor, and he called you ' dear lady,' and sometimes he would take hold of your watch-chain and finger it as he talked to you. But he was awfully clever, I believe. · He wrote reviews and very difficult poetry that didn't rhyme. Anita was generally mellifluous to him and she quoted him a good deal. She turned to him with just the same smile—

" Ah, of course ! You've met John Carey too."

" For my sins, dear lady—for my sins."

" Not the same sins, surely," breathed the blonde lady.

" As the virtuous Carey's ? Don't be rude to me ! It's a fact—the man's a churchwarden. He carries a little tin plate on Sundays! Didn't you tell me so, Anita? No—we give her a year. Don't we, Anita?"

"But what did she marry him for?" wailed the Baxter girl.

They all laughed.

"Copy, dear lady, copy!" Mr. Flood was enjoying himself. "Why will you have ideals? Carey was a new type."

"But she needn't have married him!" insisted the Baxter girl. The argument was evidently an old one.

"She, if I read her aright, could have dispensed with the ceremony, but the churchwarden had his views. Obviously! Can't you imagine him—all whiskers and wedding-ring?"

"But I thought he was clean-shaven! I thought he was good-looking!" I sympathized with the Baxter girl's dismay.

"Ah—I speak in parables——"

"You do hate him, don't you?" said Miss Howe with her wide, benevolent smile. "Now, I wonder——"

Mr. Flood flushed into disclaimers, while the woman beside him looked at Miss Howe with half-closed eyes.

"I? How could I? Our orbits don't touch. *I* approved, I assure you. An invaluable experience for our Madala! A year of wedded love, another of wedded boredom, and then — a master-piece,

21

dear people! Madala Grey back to us, a giantess refreshed. Gods! what a book it will be!"

" I wonder," said Miss Howe vaguely.

Anita answered her with that queer movement of the head that always reminded me of a pouncing lizard.

" No need! I've watched Madala Grey's career from the beginning."

" For this I maintain—" Mr. Flood ignored her— " *Eden Walls* and *Ploughed Fields* may be amazing (*The Resting-place* I cut out. It's an indiscretion. Madala caught napping) but they're preliminaries, dear people! mere preliminaries, believe me."

" I sometimes wonder——" Miss Howe made me think of Saladin's cushion in *The Talisman*. She always went on so softly and imperviously with her own thoughts—" Suppose now, that she's written herself out, and knows it?"

The Baxter girl gave a little gasp of horrified appreciation.

" So the marriage——?"

" An emergency exit."

But Anita pitied them aloud—

" It shows how little you know Madala, either of you."

" Does anyone? Do you?"

Anita smiled securely.

" The type's clear, at least." Mr. Flood looked round the circle. His eyes shone. " *Une grande amoureuse*—that I've always maintained. Carey may be the first—but he won't be the last."

"Is he the first? How did she come to write *The Resting-place* then? Tell me that!" Anita thrust at him with her forefinger and behind her, in the corner I saw the gesture duplicated.

"So I will when I've read the new book, dear lady."

"If ever it writes itself," Miss Howe underlined him.

"As to that—I give her a year, as I say. Once this business is over—" his voice mellowed into kindliness—" and good luck to her, dear woman——"

"Ah, good luck!" said Miss Howe and smiled at him.

"Once it's over, I say——"

"But she *will* be all right, won't she?" said the Baxter girl.

"I should certainly have been told——" began Anita.

Miss Howe harangued them—

"Have you ever known Madala Grey fail yet? She'll be all right. She'll pull it off—triumphantly. You see! But as for the book—if it comes——"

"When it comes," corrected Mr. Flood.

"What's that?" said Anita sharply.

There was a sound in the passage, a heavy sound of feet. It caught at my heart. It was a sound that I knew. They had come tramping up the stairs like that when they fetched away Mother.

Thud—stumble—thud! I shivered. But as the
steps came nearer they belonged to but one man.
The door opened and the fog and the man entered
together. Everyone turned to him with a queer
long flash of faces.

" Kent ! " cried Anita, welcoming him. Then her
voice changed. " Kent! What's wrong? What
is it ? "

He shut the door behind him and stood, his back
against it, staring at us, like a man stupified.

The Baxter girl broke in shrilly—

" He's wired. He's had a wire ! " She pointed
at his clenched hand.

Then he, too, looked down at his own hand. His
fingers relaxed slowly and a crush of red and grey
paper slid to the floor.

" A son," he said dully.

" Ah ! " A cry from the corner by the fire eased
the tension. Great-aunt Serle was clapping her
hands together. Her face was wrinkled all over
with delight. " The good girl ! The pretty——
And a son too ! A little son ! Oh, the good girl ! "

Anita turned on her, her voice like a scourge—

" Be quiet, Mother ! " Then—" Well, Kent ?
Well ? "

" Well ? " he repeated after her.

" Madala ? How's Madala ? What about Madala
Grey ? "

" Dead ! " he said.

Dead. The word fell amongst the group of us

LEGEND

in the circle of lamp-light, like a plummet into a
pool. *Dead.* For an instant one could hear the
blank drop of it. Then we broke up into gestures
and little cries, into a babel of dismay and concern
and rather horrible excitement.

Instinctively I separated myself from them. It
was neither bad news nor good news to me, but it
recalled to me certain hours, and they—it was as
if they enjoyed the importance of bereavement.
Anita talked. Miss Howe was gulping, and dabbing
at her eyes. The Baxter girl kept on saying—
' Dead ? ' ' Dead ? ' under her breath, and with
that wide nervous smile that you sometimes see on
people's faces when they are far enough away from
laughter. Great-aunt had shrunk into her corner.
I could barely see her. The blonde lady had her
hand on her heart and was panting a little, as if she
had been running, and yet, as always, she watched
Mr. Flood. He had pulled out a note-book and a
fountain-pen and was shaking at it furiously, while
his little eyes flickered from one to another—even
to me. I felt his observance pursue me to the
very edge of the ring of light, and drop again,
baulked by the dazzle, as I slipped past him into the
swinging shadows beyond. It's odd how lamp-
light cuts a room in two : I could see every corner
of the light and shadow alike, and even the outer
room was not too dim for me to move about it
easily; but to those directly under the lamp I
knew I had become all but invisible, a blur among

25

the other blurs that were curtains and pictures
and chairs. They remembered me as little as,
absorbed and clamorous, they remembered the man
who had brought them their news, and then had
brushed his way through question and comment to
the deep alcove of the window in the outer room
and there stood, rigid and withdrawn, staring out
through the uncurtained pane at the solid night
beyond. I could not see his face, only the outline
of a big and clumsy body, and a hand that twitched
and fumbled at the tassel of the blind.

And all the while Anita, white as paper, was
talking, talking, talking, saying how great the shock
was, and how much Miss Grey had been to her—a
stream of sorrow and self-assertion. It was just
as if she said—' Don't forget that this is far worse
for me than for any of you. Don't forget——'

But the others went on with their own thoughts.

" Dead ? Gone ? It's not possible." Miss Howe
was all blubbered and deplorable. " What shall we
do without her ? "

" Yes—that's it ! " The Baxter girl edged-in
her chair to her like a young dog asking for comfort.

" For that matter, from the point of view of
literature," Anita's voice grated, " she died a year
ago."

" It's not possible ! That's what I say—it's not
possible ! " It was strange how even the Baxter
girl ignored Anita. " Dead ! I can't grasp it.
It's—it's too awful. She was so vivid."

26

LEGEND

"Awful?" Mr. Flood was biting his fingers. "Awful? Nothing of the kind. You know that Holbein cut—no, it's earlier stuff—'Death and the Lady,' crude, preposterous. And *that's* what it is. Old Bones and Madala Grey? That's not tragedy, that's farce! Farce, dear people, farce!" Then his high tripping voice broke suddenly. "Dead? Why, she wasn't thirty!"

"She was twenty-six last June," said Anita finally. "Midsummer Day. I know."

"June!" He caught it up. "Just so—June! Isn't that characteristic? Isn't that Madala all over? Of course she was born in June. She would be. She *was* June. June——

> Her lips and her roses yet maiden,
> A summer of storm in her eyes——"

Miss Howe winced.

"For God's sake don't Swinburnize, Jasper! She's not your meat. Oh, I want to cry—I want to cry! Dead—at twenty-six——"

"In child-bed," finished Anita bitterly, and her voice made it an unclean and shameful end.

Mr. Flood's glance felt its way over her, hatefully. It never lifted to her face.

"Of course from your point of view, dear lady——" he began, and smiled as he made his little bow of attention.

I thought him insolent, and so, I believe, did Miss Howe. She lifted her head sharply and I thought she would have spoken; but Anita gave her no time.

27

LEGEND

There was always a sort of thick-skinned valliance about Anita.

" Oh, but you all know my point of view. She knew it herself. I never concealed it. You know how I devoted myself—"

" A bye-word, a bye-word ! " said Miss Howe under her breath.

" —but not so much to her as to her gift. I should never allow a personal sentiment to overpower me. I haven't the time for it. But she had the call, she had the gift, and because she had it I say, as I have always said, that for Madala Grey, marriage——"

" And all it implies——" Mr. Flood was still smiling.

She accepted it.

" Marriage and all that it implies was apostasy. I stand for Literature."

" And Literature," with a glance at the others, " is honoured."

They wearied me. It seemed to me that they sparked and fizzled and whirred with the sham life of machinery : and like machinery they affected me. For at first I could not hear anything but them, and then they confused and tired me, and last of all they faded into a mere wall-paper of sound, and I forgot that they were there, save that I wondered now and then, as stray sentences shrilled out of the buzz, that they were not yet oppressed into silence.

28

LEGEND

For there was grief abroad—a grief without shape, without sound, without expression—a quality, a pulsing essence, a distillation of pure pain. From some centre it rayed out, it spread, it settled upon the room, imperceptibly, like the fall of dust. It reached me. I felt it. It soaked into me. I ached with it. I could not sit quiet. I was not drawn, I was impelled. *Dead*—the dull bewildered voice was still in my ears. *That* I heard. But it was statement, not appeal. It was not his suffering that demanded relief, but some responding capacity for pain in me that awoke and cried out restlessly that such anguish was unlawful, beyond endurance, that still it I must, I must!

I rose. I looked round me. Then I went very softly into the outer room.

He was still standing at the window. The street lamp, level with the sill, was quenched to a yellow gloom. It lit up the wet striped branches and dead bobbins of the plane-tree beside it, and the sickly undersides of its shrivelled last leaves. I never thought a tree could look so ghastly. Against that unnatural glitter and the luminous thick air the man and the half-drawn curtain stood out in solid, unfamiliar bulk of black.

I came and stood just behind him. He was so big that I only reached his shoulder. He may have heard me : I think he did; but he did not turn. I was not frightened of him. That was so queer, because as a rule I can't talk to strangers. I get nervous and red, and foolish-tongued, especially with men. Of course I knew all the usual men, the doctor at home, and the church people, and husbands that came back by the five-thirty, and now all Anita's friends, and Mr. Flood; but I never had anything to say to them or they to me. But with Kent Rehan, somehow, it was different. He was different. I never thought—'This is a strange man.' I never thought—'He doesn't know me: it's impertinent to break in upon him: what will he think?' I never thought of all that. I never thought about myself at all. I was just passionately desiring to help him and I didn't know how to do it.

I think I stood there for four or five minutes, trying to find words, opening my lips, and then catching back the phrase before a sound came, because it seemed so poor and meaningless. And all the while the Baxter girl's words were running in my head—'They say he was in love with her.'

With her—with Madala Grey. She was the key. I had the strangest pang of interest in this unknown woman. Who was she? What was she? What had she been? What had she done so to centre herself in so many, in such alien lives? What had she in common for them all? Books, books, books— *I'd* never heard of her books! And she was married. Yet the loss of her, unpossessed, could bring such a look (as he turned restlessly from the window at last) such a look to Kent Rehan's face.

LEGEND

I was filled with a sort of anger against that dead woman, and I envied her. I never saw a man look so—as if his very soul had been bruised. It was not, it was never, a weak face, and it was not a young one; yet in that instant I saw in it, and clearly, its own forgotten childhood, bewildered by its first encounter with pain. It was that fleeting look that touched me so and gave me courage, so that I found myself saying to him, very low and quickly, and with a queer authority—

" It won't always hurt so much. It will get easier. I promise you it will. It does. Truly it does. In six months—I *do* know."

He looked down at me strangely.

I went on because I had to, but it was difficult. It was desperately difficult. I could hear myself blundering and stammering, and using hateful slangy phrases that I never used as a rule.

" I had to tell you. It isn't cheek. I know—it hurts like fun. It'll be worst out of doors. You see them coming, you see them just ahead of you, and then it isn't them. But it won't always hurt so horribly. I promise you. One manages. One gets used to living with it. I know."

He looked at my black dress.

" Your husband ? "

" No. Mother."

He said no more. But he did not go away from me. We stood side by side at the window.

The voices in the other room insisted themselves

into my mind again, against my will, like the ticking
of a clock in the night. I was thinking about him,
not them. But Anita called to me to put coal on
the fire and, once among them, I did not like to go
back to him again.

They had re-grouped themselves at the hearth.
Miss Howe was in the chair with the chintz cover
that was as pink and white and blue-ribboned
as she herself. The Baxter girl crouched on the
pouf and the fire-light danced over her by fits
and starts till, what with her violet dress and her
black boy's head with the green band in it and
that orange glow upon her, she looked like one
of the posters in the Tube. The blonde lady had
pushed back her chair to the edge of the lamp-light,
so that her face was a blur and her white dress
yellow-grey. Her knees made a back for Mr. Flood
sitting cross-legged at her feet, and watching the
Baxter girl as if he admired her. Once the blonde
lady put her hand on his shoulder, and he caught it
and played with the rings on it while he listened to
her, and yet still watched the Baxter girl. She went
on whispering, her hand in his, till at last he put
back his head and caught her eye and laughed.
Then she leaned back again as if she were satisfied.
But I thought—' How I should hate to have that
dank hair rubbing against my skirt.' Beside Mr.
Flood lay the MS. he had brought, but I think
Anita had forgotten it. She, sitting at the table
in her high-backed chair (she never lolled), was still

talking, indeed they were all talking about this
Madala Grey. Anita's voice was as pinched as her
face.

" Oh, I knew from the first what it would be !
She could never do anything by halves. She had
no moderation. The writing, the work, all that
made her what she was, tossed aside, for a whim,
for a madness, for a man. I can't help it—it makes
me bitter."

" Do you grudge it her so ? " The Baxter girl
looked at her wonderingly. " I kicked at it too,
of course. We all did, didn't we ? But now, I
like to think how happy she looked the last time she
came here. Do you remember ? I liked that blue
frock. And the scarf with the roses—I gave her
that. Liberty. She was thin though. She always
worked too hard. Poor Madala ! Heigh-ho, the
gods are jealous gods."

Anita stared in front of her.

" Just gods. She served two masters. She was
bound to pay."

" You are hard," said the Baxter girl in a low
voice.

Miss Howe rocked herself.

" But don't you know how she feels ? I do.
It's the helplessness——"

Anita's pale eye met and held her glance as if
she resented that sympathy. Then, as if indeed
she were suddenly grown weak, she acquiesced.

" I suppose so. Yes, it's the helplessness. ' If

this didn't happen '—' If that weren't so '—Little things, little things—and they govern one. A broken doll—a cowslip ball—stronger than all my strength. And she needn't have met Carey. It was just a chance. If I'd known—that day! I used to ask her questions, just to make her talk. I remember asking her about her old home—more to set her off than anything. I said I'd like to see it some day. It was true. I was interested. But it was only to make her talk. But she—oh, you know how she foamed up about a thing. ' My old home! Would you, Anita? Would you like to come? Wouldn't it bore you, Anita? It's all spoiled, you know. But I go down now and then. Nobody remembers me. It's like being a ghost. Oh, I *feel* for ghosts. Would you really like to come? Shall we go soon? Shall we go today?' And then, of course, down we go. And then we meet Carey. And then the play begins."

Miss Howe shook her head.

" Ends."

Anita accepted it.

" Ends. Then the play ends." And then, frowning—" If I'd known that day—if I'd known! I was warned, too. That's strange. I've never thought of it from that day to this. If I were an old wife now——" She shivered.

" What happened? " said the Baxter girl curiously.

" Oh well, off we went! We had a carriage to ourselves. I was glad. I thought she might talk."

"And you always tried to make her talk," said Miss Howe softly.

Anita went on without answering her.

"She grew quite excited as we travelled down, talking about her 'youth.' She always spoke as if she were a hundred."

"She put something into that youth of hers, I shouldn't wonder," said Miss Howe.

"She did. The things she told me that day. I knew she had been in America, but I never dreamed—— She landed there, if you please, without a penny in her pocket, without a friend in the world."

"I never understood why she went to America," said Miss Howe. "I asked her once."

"What did she say?" said Anita curiously.

"To make her fortune. But I never got any details out of her."

"Didn't you know?" said Anita. "Her people emigrated. The father failed. It happened when Madala was eighteen, and she and her mother persuaded him, expecting him, literally, to make their fortunes. The mother seems to have been an erratic person. Irish, I believe. Beautiful. Extravagant. I have always imagined that it was her extravagance—but Madala and the husband seem to have adored her. I remember Madala saying once that her father had been born unlucky, 'except when he married Mother!' I suspect, myself, that that was the beginning of his ill-luck.

Anyhow, when the crash came, they gathered together what they had and started off on some romantic notion of the mother's to make their fortune farming. America. Steerage. The *Sylvania.*"

" *Sylvania?* That's familiar. What was it? A collision, wasn't it?"

" No, that was the *Empress of Peru.* The *Sylvania* caught fire in mid-ocean—a ghastly business. There were only about fifty survivors. Both her people were drowned."

" Oh, that's what she meant," began Miss Howe, " that time at the Academy. We were looking at a storm-scape, and she said—' People don't know. It's not like that. They wouldn't try to paint it if they knew.' She was quite white. Of course I never dreamed—— Poor old Madala! Well, what happened?"

" Oh, she reached America in what she stood up in. There was a survivors' fund, of course, but money melts in a city when you're strange to it."

" Couldn't she have come back to England?"

" I believe she had relations over here, but her mother had quarrelled with them all in turn. They didn't appreciate her mother and that was the unforgivable sin for Madala. She'd have starved sooner than ask them to help her. I shouldn't wonder if she did, too!—half starve anyway. I shouldn't wonder if those first bare months haven't revenged themselves at last."

LEGEND

"Oh, if one had known!" began the Baxter girl. "How is it that no-one ever knows—or cares?"

"You? You were a schoolgirl. Who had heard of her in those days? But she made friends. There was a girl, a journalist, who had been sent to interview the survivors. She seems to have helped her in the beginning. She found her a lodging—oh, can't you see how she uses that lodging in *Eden Walls*?—and gave her occasional hack jobs, typing, and now and then proof-reading. Then she got some work taken, advertisement work, little articles on soaps and scents and face-creams that she used to illustrate herself. She was comically proud of them. She kept them all."

"I suppose in her spare time she was already working at *Eden Walls*?"

"No. I asked her. And she said—'Oh no, I was too miserable. Oh, Anita, I *was* miserable.' And then she began again telling funny stories about her experiences. No, she was back in England before she began *Eden Walls*. However, she seems to have made quite a little income at last, even to have saved. And then, just when she began to see her way before her to a sort of security, then she threw it all up and came home."

"Just like Madala! But why?"

"Heaven knows! Home-sick, she said."

"But she hadn't got a home!"

"It was England—the English country—the

87

south country—the Westering Hill country. She used to talk about it like—like a lover."

" Isn't that more probable ? " said Mr. Flood.

" What ? "

" A lover ? "

" Carey ? "

" Not necessarily Carey."

Anita looked at him with a certain approval.

" Ah—so you've thought of that too? Now what exactly do you base it on ? "

He shrugged and smiled.

" Delightfullest—my thoughts are thistledown.'

" But you have your theory ? " She pinned him down. " I see that you too have your theory."

" Our theory." He bowed.

" You've got wits, Jasper."

" What are you two driving at ? " Miss Howe fidgeted.

" We're evolving a theory—a theory of Madala Grey. Who lived in the south country, Anita ? "

" Carey, for that matter."

" Matters not. She didn't come home for Carey. You can't make books without copy. Not her sort of book. Any more than you can make bricks without straw. But she didn't make her bricks from his straw, that I'll swear."

" No, she didn't come home for Carey," said Anita. " I tell you, that was the day she met him. It's barely a year ago. She had made her name twice over by then. She was already casting about for

38

LEGEND

her third plot. I think it was that that made her so restless. She'd grown very restless. But she certainly didn't come home for Carey."

" Then why ? "

" Homesick."

" That's absurd."

" I'm telling you what she said. She insisted on it. She used a queer phrase. She said—' I longed for home till my lips ached.' "

The lady with Mr. Flood stirred in her shadows.

" She didn't imagine that. That happens. That is how one longs——" She broke off.

" For home ? " he said, with that smile of his that ended at his mouth and left his eyes like chips of quartz.

She answered him slowly, him only—

" I suppose, with some women, it could be for home. If she says so—— That is what confounds one in her. She knows—she proves that she knows, in a phrase like that, things that (when one thinks of her personality) she *can't* know—couldn't know. It's inexplicable. ' Till one's lips ache '— Oh, Lord ! " She laughed harshly.

Anita looked at them uncertainly.

" Well, that's what she said. And to judge from her description Westering was something to be homesick for. I expected a paradise."

" Westering ? That's quite a town."

" Yes, I know. There's a summer colony. Madala mourned over it. She was absurd. She

39

LEGEND

raced me out of the station and up the hill, and
would scarcely let me look about me till we were
at the top, because the lower end of the village had
been built over. It might have been the sack of
Rome to hear her—‘ Asphalt paths ! Disgraceful !
The grocer used to have *blue* blinds. They’ve
spoiled the village green.’ And so it went on until
we reached Upper Westering.”

“ Oh, where they live now ? ”

“ Yes. And then she turned to me and beamed—
‘ *This is* my *country.*’ It certainly is a pretty place.
There’s a fine view over the downs; but too hilly
for me. We climbed up and down lanes and picked
ridiculous bits of twig and green stuff till I protested. Then she took me into the churchyard.
We wandered about : very pleasant it was : such
a hot spring day, and pretty pinkish flowers—what
did she call the stuff ?—cuckoo-pint, springing from
the graves—and daffodils. Then we sat down in
the shadow of the church to eat our lunch. We
began to discuss architecture and I was growing
interested, really beginning to enjoy myself—some
of it was pre-Norman—when a man climbed over
the stile from the field behind the church, and came
down the path towards us. As he passed, Madala
looked up and he looked down, and up she jumped
in a moment. ‘ Why,’ she said, ‘ I do believe—I
do believe—’ You know that little chuckly rise in
her voice when she’s pleased—‘ I do believe it’s
you ! ’ ‘ Oh, Madala,’ I said, ‘ the sandwiches ! ! ’

40

They were in a paper on her lap, you know. She had scattered them right and left. But I might have talked to the wind. I must say he had perfectly respectable manners. He turned back at once, and smiled at her, and hesitated, and began to pick up the sandwiches, though he evidently didn't know her. 'Oh,' she said, 'don't you remember? Aren't you Dr. Carey? You mended my camel when I was little. I'm Madala!' She was literally brimming over with pleasure. But, you know, such a silly way to put it! If she had said 'Madala Grey' he would have known in a moment. There were a couple of *Eden Walls* on the bookstall as we went through. I saw them. However, he remembered her then. He certainly seemed pleased to see her, in his awkward way. He stood looking down at her, amused and interested. People always got so interested in Madala. Haven't you noticed it? Even people in trams. Though I thought to myself at the time—'How absurd Madala is! What can they have in common?' Yes, I thought it even then."

" Well, what had they in common ? "

" Heaven knew ! She was ten and he was twenty-five when they last met. He knew her grand-people : he had mended her dolls for her : he lived in her old home : that, according to her, was all that mattered. She said to me afterwards, I remember, 'Just imagine seeing him ! I *was* pleased to see him. He belongs in, you know.'

41

' No, Madala,' I said, ' I don't know. Such a fuss about a man you haven't seen since you were a child ! I call it affectation. It's a slight on your real friends.' ' Oh,' she said, ' but he belongs in.' She looked quite chastened. She said—' Nita, it wasn't affectation. I believe he was pleased too— honestly ! ' He was. Who wouldn't be ? You know the effect she used to make."

" What did he say ? " asked the Baxter girl.

" Oh, he looked down at her as if he were shy. Then he said—' You've a long memory, Madala ! ' Yes, he called her Madala from the first. It annoyed me. She said—' Oh, do you remember when Mother was so ill once ? You were very kind to me then.' Then she said something which amazed me. I'd known her for two years before she told me anything about that *Sylvania* tragedy, but to him she spoke at once. ' They're dead,' she said, ' Mother and Father. They're drowned. There isn't anyone.' But her voice ! It made me quite nervous. I thought she was going to break down. He said, with a stiff sort of effort—' Yes. I heard.' That was all. Nothing sympathetic. He just stood and looked at her."

" Well ? " said Miss Howe impatiently.

" Oh—nothing else. I finished picking up the sandwiches. She introduced me, but I don't think he realized who I was. It annoyed me very much that she insisted on his eating lunch with us. As I said to her afterwards, it wasn't suitable. Buns in a bag! Rut there he sat on a damp stone, (he gave Madala his overcoat to sit upon) perfectly contented. I confess I wasn't cordial. But he noticed nothing. Obtuse! That was how I summed him up from the first—obtuse! And no conversation whatever. Madala did the talking. I believe she asked after every cat and dog for twenty miles round. And her lack of reticence to a comparative stranger was amazing. She told him more about herself in half an hour than she had told me in four years. But she was an unaccountable creature.

"Yes, that's just it. One never knew what Madala would do next, and yet when she'd done it, one said—'Of course! Just what Madala *would* do!' But it wasn't like her to neglect you, Nita!"

"Oh, she noticed after a time. She began to be uncomfortable. I—withdrew myself, as it were. You know my way. She didn't like that. She tried—I will say that for her—she did try to direct the conversation towards my subjects. Useless, of course. He was, not illiterate—no, you can't say illiterate—but curiously unintellectual. Socialism now—somehow we got on to socialism. That roused him. I must say, though he expressed himself clumsily, that he had ideas. But so limited. He had never heard of Marx. Bernard Shaw was barely a name to him. Socialism—his socialism— when we disentangled it, was only another word for the proper feeding of the local infants—drains—

measles—the village schools. Beyond that he was
mute. But Madala chimed in with details of
American slum life, and roused him at once. They
grew quite eloquent. But not one word, if you
please, of her own work. Anything and everything but her work. He did ask her what she was
doing. 'Oh,' said she in an offhand way, 'I
scribble. Stories.' And then—'It earns money,
and it kills time.' Yes, that's exactly how she put
it. 'Madala!' I said, 'that's not the spirit—'
I'd never heard her use such a tone before. She
had such high ideals of art. It jarred me. I
thought that she ought to have known better. But
she looked at me in such a curious way—defiant
almost. She said—'It's my own spirit, Nita. Oh,
let me have a holiday!' And at that up she
jumped and left us sitting there, and wandered off
to the stile and was over it in a second. We sat
still. The hedge hid her. Then we heard her
call—'Cowslips! Oh, cowslips!' I thought he
would go when she called, but he sat where he
was, listening. It was one of those hot, still days,
you know. There was a sort of spell on things.
There were bees about. We heard a cart roll up
the road. I wanted to get up and talk, make some
kind of diversion, and yet I couldn't. We heard
her call again—'Hundreds of cowslips! I'm going
to make a cowslip ball.' Her voice sounded far
away, but very clear. And there was a scent of
may in the air, and dust—an intoxicating smell.

LEGEND

It made me quite sleepy. It was just as if time stood still. Three o'clock's a drowsy time, I suppose. And he never stirred—just sat there stupidly. But I was too sleepy to be bored with him. Presently back she came. She had picked up her skirt and her petticoat showed—it war that lavender silk you gave her, Lila. So unsuitable, you know, on those dirty roads. And her skirt was full of cowslips. She was just a dark figure against the sky until she was close to us; but then, I thought that she looked pretty, extremely pretty. Bright cheeks, you know, and her eyes so blue——"

" Grey—" said Mr. Flood, " the grey eyes of a goddess."

" They looked blue, and she didn't look like a goddess. She looked like a little girl. Well, there she stood, with her grey skirt and her lavender silk, and her cowslips—you know they have a sweet smell, cowslips, a very sweet smell—and tumbled them all down on the tombstone. Then she wanted string. Carey seemed to wake up at that. He'd been looking at her as if he had dreamed her. He produced string. He was that sort of man. Then she made her cowslip ball. I held one end of the string and he held the other, and she nipped the stalks off the flowers and strung them athwart it. That is the way to make a cowslip ball."

" Nita, I love you!" cried Miss Howe for the second time, and the others laughed.

She stopped. She stiffened.

LEGEND

"I don't know what you mean."

"Ne' mind! Go on!"

She said offendedly—

"There's nothing more to tell. We got up and came away."

But as we sat silently by, still waiting, the story-teller crept back into her face.

"Oh, yes—" up went her forefinger. "It was then that it happened. We went stumbling over the graves, round to the east end, to see the lepers' window, a particularly interesting one. Ruskin mentions it. Yes, Carey came with us. There's a little bit of bare lawn under the window before the stones begin again, and as we crossed it Madala gave a kind of shuddering start. He said—'Cold?' smiling at her. She shivered again, in spite of her-self as it were, for she'd been joking and laughing, and said—'Someone must be walking over my grave.' And at that he gave her such a look, and said loudly in a great rough voice—'Rubbish! don't talk such rubbish!' Really, you know, the tone! And I thought to myself then as I've thought many times since—'At heart the man's a bully—that's what the man is.' But Madala laughed. We didn't stay long after that. The window was a disappointment—restored. There was nothing further to see and Madala was quite right—it was chilly. The sky had clouded over and there was a wind. I thought it time to go. Madala made no objection. She had grown curiously quiet. She

tired easily, you know. And he didn't say another
word. Quite time to go. I thought we might try
for the earlier train, so we went off at last in a
hurry. No, he didn't come with us : we shook
hands at the gate. And when I looked back a
minute later he had turned away. We caught our
train."

There was a little pause that Miss Howe ended.

" Queer ! " she said.

Anita stared at them. Her hands twitched.

" Oh, I'm a practical person, but—' You're
walking on my grave,' she said. And there or
thereabouts, I suppose, she'll lie."

" Coincidence," said Mr. Flood quickly.

" Of course. I never thought of it again. Nor
did Madala for that matter, though she was quiet
enough in the train. There she sat, looking out of
the window and smiling to herself. But then she
was always like that after any little excitement,
very quiet for an hour, re-living it—literally. I
think, you know," she hesitated, " that that was
the secret of her genius. Her genius was her
memory. *She liked whate'er she looked on——*"

" And her looks were certainly everywhere," said
the blonde lady in her drawling voice.

" Just so. But it didn't end there. She remembered. She remembered uncannily. She was like
a child picking up pebbles from the beach every
holiday, and spending all the rest of its year polish-
ing. She turned them into jewels. The process

47

used to fascinate me—professionally, you know.
You could see her mind at work on some trifling
incident, fidgeting with it, twisting it, dropping it,
picking it up again, till one wearied. And then a
year later, or two years, or three years, or ten years
maybe, you'll pick up a novel or a story, and there
you'll find it, cut, graved, polished, set in diamonds,
but—the same pebble, if one has the wit to see."

" Well, what did she say?" Miss Howe cut
through the theory impatiently.

Anita frowned. She disliked being hurried.

" Oh, that day? very little. I was surprised.
She usually enjoyed pouring herself out to me. But
no, she just sat and smiled. It irritated me. ' What
is it, Madala?' I said at last. She stared at me as
if she had never seen me before. ' I don't know,'
she said in her vague way. And then—' Wasn't it
a lovely day?' I waited. I knew she would go
on sooner or later. Presently she said—' That stone
we sat on *was* damp. He was quite right.' Then
she said, thinking aloud as it were—' You know,
if a man has a really pleasant voice, I like it better
than women's voices. It's so steady.' And then—
' What did you think of him, Anita?' "

Miss Howe chuckled.

" And you said?"

" Oh, I said what I could. I didn't want to hurt
her feelings. It was so obvious that the place and
everyone in it was beglamoured for her. I said
that he seemed a worthy, harmless person, or some-

LEGEND

thing to that effect. I forget exactly how I phrased
it—I was tactful, of course. Oh, I remember, I said
that she ought to put him into a book—that the old
country doctors were disappearing, like the farmers
and the parsons. I'm sure I appeared interested.
But all she said was—'Old? He's not old. Would
you call him old?' 'That was a figure of speech,'
I said. 'I was thinking of the type. But all the
same you can't describe him as young, Madala.'
'Oh, he's not a boy,' she said. 'No-one ever said
he was a *boy*.' She didn't say any more. But just
as we were getting out at Victoria she cried—'My
cowslips! Anita, my cowslips! I've forgotten my
cowslip ball.' I told her that it wouldn't have
lasted anyway, with the stalks nipped off so short.
But she looked as if she had lost a kingdom."

"I believe I know that cowslip ball." Miss
Howe looked amused. "*A* cowslip ball, anyway.
She had one sent to her once when I was there.
I thought it was from her slum children."

"Yes, he sent it on." My cousin went on quickly
with her own story. "How he knew the address
puzzled me. Her publishers wouldn't have given
it and I know she didn't."

"Telephone book," said the Baxter girl, as one
experienced.

"Ah, possibly. I went round to her that morn
ing, and—yes, you were there, Lila," she conceded,
"for I remember I wondered how Madala could
compose herself to work with anyone else in the

49

room. I always left her to herself when she stayed with me."

" She didn't mind me," said Miss Howe firmly.

" She always said that she didn't, I know. And of course I know that it is possible to withdraw oneself as it were, but I confess I disapproved. Her room was . regular clearing-house in those days. Oh, not you particularly, Lila, but——"

" You came in yourself that morning, didn't you?" said Miss Howe very softly and sweetly.

" I was telling you so. And what did I find? Her desk littered over with string and paper and moss and damp cardboard, and that story Hooper published (it had been freshly typed only the day before) watering into purple under my eyes, while she sat and gloated over those wretched flowers. 'Madala!' I said, 'your manuscript! Really, Madala!'"

" And Madala—" Miss Howe began to laugh— " Oh, I remember now."

" What did Madala say?" demanded the Baxter girl.

" It wasn't like her." Anita fidgeted. " She knew how I disliked the modern manner."

" But she said," Miss Howe caught it up—

" I don't know what possessed her," said my cousin with a rush. " She actually stamped her foot at me. Yes, she did, and then held out her wretched posy and said—' Oh, damn the manu-script, Nita! Smell!'"

LEGEND

" What did Nita do ? " enquired the blonde lady softly of Miss Howe.

" Sniffed," Mr. Flood struck in. " Obviously ! Satisfied Madala and relieved her own feelings. That is called tact."

" And just then, you know," Miss Howe glanced over her shoulder and lowered her voice, " *he* came in."

" Kent ? " The lady with Mr. Flood did not lower her voice. I believe she wanted him to hear. She was like a curious child poking at a hurt beastie. Her smile was infantine as she looked across at him. But the man at the window never stirred.

" Sh ! " Miss Howe frowned at her. And then, still whispering—" Yes, don't you remember ? he had his studio in the same block all that year. He always came across to Madala when he wanted a sardine tin opened, or change for his gas, or someone to sit to him."

" Someone was saying that he couldn't keep a model." Mr. Flood glanced at them in turn.

Miss Howe flushed surprisingly.

" It's not that. You ought to know better, Jasper. It's only that he's exigeant—never knows how the time goes, and—" she lowered her voice still more, " and Madala spoilt him. She could sit by the hour looking like a Madonna, and getting all her own head-work done, and never stirring a hair. Of course he doesn't like the shilling an hour type after her."

LEGEND

"I know, I know! The explanation is quite unnecessary." He smiled and waved his hand.

"Then why——?" She was still flushed and annoyed.

"One gets at other people's views. I merely wondered how the—er—partnership appeared to your—er—intelligence. Now I know."

"She did spoil him." Anita disregarded them. "The time she wasted on him! In he came, you know, that day, and she went to meet him with the cowslips still in her hand, and shielding her eyes from the sun. That room of hers got all the morning sun."

"What did she wear—the blue dress?" The Baxter girl was like a child being told a story.

"I forget. Anyway he stood looking her up and down till she reddened and began to laugh at him. And then he said—'And cowslips too! What luck! Come along! Come *along!*' 'Oh, my good man!' I said, 'she's in the middle of her writing!' But it was useless to expostulate. He wanted her and so she went. I heard him as he dragged her off. 'Madala, I've got such a notion!' No, it was the great fault of her character, I consider, that she could never deny anyone, not even for her work's sake. Still, I suppose one had to forgive it in that case, for that was the beginning, you know, of *The Spring Song*. She is painted just as she stood there that morning, literally gilded over with sunshine, and the flowers in her hands."

"It's the best thing he's ever done, isn't it?" said the Baxter girl.

"Best thing? It's a master-piece. It's Madala Grey."

"When is he going to show it?" said Mr. Flood. Anita shrugged.

"Heaven knows! He insists that it isn't finished. I believe he sits and prays over it. He was annoyed that Madala took me there one day. You know how touchy he is."

"He won't show it now," said the blonde lady.

"Why not? Why not?" Anita hovered, on the pounce, like a cat over a bowl of goldfish, and like a fish the blonde lady glided out of reach.

"And *she* asks!" she appealed to the others. Anita frowned.

"You're cryptic."

"Well, wasn't there a certain—rivalry? You should have a fellow-feeling."

"Oh—" she resented quickly, "Kent always wanted to keep her to himself, if you mean that."

The blonde lady smiled.

"And now he keeps her to himself. I mean just that. I go by your account, of course. *I* haven't glimpsed *The Spring Song*."

"So that started it." The Baxter girl mused aloud. "I think that's romantic now—to make a famous picture and to pick up one's husband, all in twenty-four hours."

"'Pick up!'"

LEGEND

" You know what I mean—fall in love."

" ' Fall in love ! ' "

" Nita, don't trample." Miss Howe threw the Baxter girl a cigarette.

" I only mean—it was romantic, meeting like that so long ago and nobody knowing a word until just before they were married, except you, Miss Serle. And I don't believe you guessed ? " She questioned her with defiant eyebrows.

" How could I guess what never happened ? ' In love ! ' I suppose it deceived some good folks."

" It wasn't so long ago," Miss Howe soothered them. She had a funny little way of slipping people into another subject if she thought that they sounded quarrelsome. ' Let's be comfortable ! ' was written all over her. And yet she could scratch. I think that a great many women are like Miss Howe.

" Long ago ? Of course not ! " Anita picked it up at once. " How long is it ? A year ? Eighteen months ? April, wasn't it ? She wrote *The Resting-place* in the next three months. Scamped. I shall always say so. She was three years over *Ploughed Fields*. Yes, April began it. *The Resting-place* was out for the Christmas sales. She married him at Easter. And now it's November. The year's not gone. But Madala Grey is gone."

" Where ? " said the Baxter girl intensely.

" Don't ! " said Miss Howe.

But the Baxter girl looked as if she couldn't stop herself.

54

LEGEND

" We—we put her into the past tense—d'you notice how easily we're doing it already?—but —is she less alive to you, less lovable, less Madala Grey to you, because of a telegram and a funeral service? is she?"

" No," said Miss Howe. " If you put it like that— no."

" Yes," said Mr. Flood. " When you put it like that—yes."

" She must be somewhere," argued the Baxter girl. " She can't just stop."

" Why not?" said Mr. Flood, with his bored smile.

" She can't. I feel it," she said with her hand at her heart and her large eyes on him.

" I don't," he said to her, and he lost his smile. " ' Dust to dust——' "

The woman behind him moved restlessly.

" Jasper, *dear!* How trite!"

" But the spirit?" said the Baxter girl, " the spirit?"

Nobody answered. The little blue flames on the hearth capered and said ' Chik-chik!' Anita shivered.

" The room's getting cold," she said sharply. And then—" Jenny, is that door open? There's such a draught."

I got up and went to see. But the door was shut. When I came back they were talking again. Anita was answering the Baxter girl.

" Yes, I stayed there once. A pretty place. The sort of place she would choose. All roses. No conveniences. And what with the surgery and the socialism, the poor seemed to be always with us. Only one servant——"

" She *ought* to have made money," said Miss Howe.

" Oh, the first two books were a *succès d'estime*, I wept over her contract. She did make a considerable amount of money on *The Resting-place*. But it was all put by for the child. She told me so. He, you know, a poor man's doctor! She told me that too—flung it at me. She had an extravagant way of talking, manner more than anything, of course, but to hear her you would almost think she was proud of the life they led. She was always unpractical."

" I'd like to have gone down there once," said Miss Howe. " If I'd known—heigh-ho ! "

" I—I wished I hadn't gone," said Anita slowly. " It wasn't a success."

" The husband, I suppose," the Baxter girl hinted delicately.

" No, I hardly saw him. It was Madala herself. Changed. Affectionate—she was always that to me but——I remember sitting with her once. We had been talking, about Aphra Behn I believe, and she had grown flushed and had begun to stammer a little. You know her way ? "

" I know." The Baxter girl leaned forward eagerly.

56

LEGEND

"And she was tracing a parallel between the development of the novel and the growth of the woman's movement—her old vein. Brilliant, she was. And all at once she stopped and began staring in front of her. You know that trick she had of frowning out her thoughts. I was careful not to interrupt. I knew something big was coming. She could be—prophetic, sometimes. At last she said in a worried sort of way—' I've a dreadful feeling that we're out of coffee and it's early closing.' No, I'm not exaggerating—her very words. And then some long rigmarole about Carey's appetite, and that if she made the coffee black strong she could persuade him to take more milk with it. Oh—pitiful! And in a moment she'd dashed off on a three-mile walk to the next village where there was a grocer that did open on Wednesdays. Oh, it was most pathetic. It made me realize the effect that he was having on her—stultifying! I always did dislike him."

"Well, I don't know," said Miss Howe.

"Just so—you don't know. Naturally, you were not so intimate with Madala. Well, that very afternoon, I remember, he came in at tea-time. That was unusual : he was generally late for seven-thirty dinner, and then he didn't change. I used to wonder how Madala allowed it. Well, as I was telling you, he came in, stamping through the hall, calling to her, and when he opened the drawing-room door and found that she was out, you should have seen

57

his look! Sour! No other word! And off he
went at once to meet her, on his bicycle, though I
was prepared to give him tea. They didn't come
back for hours. In fact I had gone up to change.
I saw them from the window, coming up the drive.
And there was Madala Grey, perched on *his* bicycle,
with a great bunch of that white parsley that grows
in the hedges, and a string bag dangling down,
while he steadied her, and both of them *talking!*
and as he helped her off, she kissed him—in front of
the kitchen windows. And, if you please, not a
word of apology to me. All she said was—why
hadn't I seen that he had some tea before he went
after her? I think it's the only time I've ever
seen Madala annoyed. No, you can't say the marriage improved her." She paused. " It was so
unlike her," she meditated, " as if I could help it!
You know, I'd always thought her so considerate.
Carey's influence, of course. Oh," she cried out
suddenly and angrily, " I've got nothing against
Carey. I'm not prejudiced. But if he'd been the
sort of man one could approve—someone—" Her
eye wandered from Kent Rehan to Mr. Flood—
" but he was dragging her down——"

Miss Howe shook her head.

" Anita, you're wrong. I've only met him a
couple of times but I liked what I saw of him.
An honest, straightforward sort of person. Oh,
not clever, of course. He'd have bored me in
a week——"

" Ah ? " said the woman behind Mr. Flood.

" Oh yes, dull—distinctly. But I had the impression that if I'd been one of his patients I should have done everything he told me to do."

Anita shrugged.

" Oh, I've no doubt he had every virtue, but it's idle to pretend that he made any attempt to appreciate Madala Grey."

" You don't suggest that the man didn't love his wife, do you ? " said Miss Howe in her downright way.

" I suggest nothing. But the fact remains—I give it for what it is worth—but the fact does remain that John Carey has never read one of her books—not one ! "

" What ? " The Baxter girl's mouth opened and stayed so.

" You don't intend to say——" began Mr. Flood.

" I don't believe it," said Miss Howe contemptuously.

" Why not ? I've known a man jealous of his wife before now. I suppose he knew enough to know that she had the brains." The blonde lady was smiling.

Anita shook her head reluctantly.

" Jealousy ? Hm—it might have been, of course. But I didn't get that impression. I believe that it was a perfectly genuine lack of interest."

" Yes, but I don't believe it. How d'you know he didn't ? It's not a thing he'd own to. Who told you ? "

LEGEND

" Madala. Madala herself. She used to make a joke of it."

" She never showed when she was hurt," said the Baxter girl emotionally.

" Yes, but it almost seemed as if she were not hurt, as if her—her sensitiveness, her better feelings, had been blunted. I've known her use it as a *weapon* almost," said Anita conscientiously recollecting. " He—that annoyed me so—he was very peremptory with her sometimes, most rude in his manner. Of course, you know, she *was* dreamy. Not that that excused him for a moment. I remember a regular scene——"

" Before you?" Miss Howe cast instant doubt upon it.

" My room was next to theirs. I could hear them through the wall. I can assure you that he stormed at her in a most ungentlemanly way—"

" What about?" said the Baxter girl breathlessly.

" Something about his razors. A parcel had come by the early post, and just because she had cut the string—but I couldn't follow it all. He was a man who was easily irritated by trifles. Well, as I say, after he had raged at her for five minutes or more, till I could have gone in and spoken to him myself, all that that patient woman said, was— ' Darling, have you begun *Eden Walls* yet?' I tell you the man never said another word."

" He didn't prevent her writing, did he?" said Miss Howe.

LEGEND

" There's no doubt that he discouraged her. He was selfish. It was his wretched doctoring all day long—and you know how sensitive Madala was. I did persuade her to do some work while I was staying with them, but I soon saw that it was labour thrown away. Her heart wasn't in it. When it wasn't Carey it was the baby clothes. For the sake of her reputation," her voice hardened, " it's as well that she has died when she has."

" Anita ! "

" I mean it." She was quick and fierce. " Do you think it was a little thing for me to see that pearl of great price—oh, not Madala Grey ! I grew to hate her almost, that new Madala Grey—but the gift within her, her great, blazing genius—flung away, trampled on——"

Miss Howe turned her head in slow denial.

" No, Anita ! Not genius. Charm, if you like. Talent, as much as you please. But Madala Grey wasn't a genius, and she knew it."

Anita flung up her head.

" She will be when I've done with her. She will be when I've written the *Life*."

" Ah, the poor child ! " said Great-aunt startlingly.

Anita never heeded. She was wrapt away in some cold passion of her own, a passion that amazed me. I had always thought of her as what she looked, an ordered, steely woman, all brain and will ; yet now of a sudden she revealed herself, a creature convulsed, writhing in flames. But they were cold flames. Cold fire, is there such a thing? Ice burns. There is phosphorus. There is the light of stars. I know what I mean if only I had the words. Star-fire—that's it. She was like a dead star. She warmed no-one, she only burned herself up.

It was the impression of a moment. When I looked again it was as if I had been withdrawn from a telescope.' She was herself once more. The volcano had shrunk to a diamond twinkle, to a tiny, gesticulating creature with a needle tongue. It was bewildering: while I listened to her I was still thinking—' Yes, but which is Anita? Diamond or star? What makes the glitter? Frost or flame?'

But that blonde woman in the shadows went off into noiseless laughter that woke the dragons and stirred Mr. Flood to an upward glance. Then he hunched himself closer against her knees, his chin low on his chest, so that his tiny beard and mouth and eyes were like triangles standing on their points. The pose gave him a glinting air of mockery and yet, somehow, you did not feel that he was amused. You only felt—' Oh, he's practised that at a looking-glass.'

He drawled out—

" The *Life*, dear lady? Enlighten our darkness."

" That," came the murmur behind him, " is precisely what she is going to do. How dense you are, Jasper!"

LEGEND

And at the same moment from Miss Howe—

" Be quiet, you two! Tell us, Anita! A life
of her? Is that it? Ah, well, I always suspected
your note-book. Did she know you Boswellized? "

" She? " There was the strangest mixture of
scorn and admiration in the voice. " As if one could
let her know! That was the difficulty with Madala
Grey : she wouldn't take herself seriously. She
had—" a pause and a search for the correct word—
" what I can only call a *perverted* sense of humour.
If she'd known that I—noted things, she'd have
been quite capable of falsifying all her opinions,
misrepresenting herself completely, just to—throw
me out, as it were. Not maliciously, I don't mean
that. But she teases," finished Anita petulantly.
" She will do it. She laughs at the wrong things.
Of course she's young still."

" Yes, she's young—now. She stays young now.
She gains that at least," said the woman in the
shadows.

Anita made a quick little sound, half titter and
half gasp.

" Oh! " she cried—and her voice was as grey as
her face—" I forgot. Do you know—I forgot!
It's going to be ghastly. I believe I shall always
be forgetting."

I glanced up at Kent Rehan. It made me realize
that I had been listening with anxiety, that I was
afraid of their expressive sentences. They had
words, those writing people. They knew what they

63

LEGEND

thought: they could say what they thought: and what they thought could hurt. I didn't want him to be hurt. I said, under my breath—

" Oh, why do you stay here? They aren't your sort."

But he had heard nothing. He was poring over the long tassel of the blind, weaving it into a six-strand plait. I couldn't help watching his fingers. He had the most beautiful hands that I've ever seen on a man. They looked like two alive and independent creatures. They looked as if they could do anything they chose, whether he were there to superintend or not. And he was miles away. I was glad. Anita's voice was rising like a dreary wind.

" Just that is so strange. All the time I've known her I've thought of her in the past tense. Her moods, her ways, her actions, were finished things to me—chapters of the *Life*. I *wrote* her all the time. But now, when she *is* mine, as it were, now that she exists only in my notes and papers and remembrance of her, now it comes that I'm shaken. I can't think of her as a subject any more. I shall be wanting her—herself. I can't think clearly. It's frightening me, the work there is ahead of me. Because I've got to do it without her. She's lying dead down there in Surrey—now—at this minute. And there's that man—and a child. One's over-whelmed. It's so cruel. The only creature who **ever** cared for me. Think of Madala, quite still,

64

not answering, not lighting up when you speak to
her, staring at the ceiling, staring at her own coffin-
lid. In two days she'll be under the ground. Do
you ever think what that means—burial—the
corruption—the——"

"Stop it, Nita!" Miss Howe's movement blotted
out my cousin's face. "Do you hear? I can't
stand it. Here—drink some coffee. Jasper! Say
something!" I heard the coffee-cup dance in its
saucer.

There came Aunt Serle's anxious quaver—

"Anita! Nita! What's the matter, my dear?
What's the matter with my daughter?"

Nobody answered. She was like a tortoise as
she poked her head from the hood of her chair.

"Jenny!" she called cautiously. "Jenny!"

I slipped across the room to her.

"What's it about, Jenny? Eh? Speak up, my
dear! Not crying, is she? Temper, that's it.
Don't say I said so."

"It's all right, Auntie. She—they—it's the bad
news. It's upset them all."

"Bad news? Fiddlesticks! Temper, I call it.
Why shouldn't the girl get married? Not much
money, but a pleasant fellow. Time for her to
settle. I said to her—'My dear, you follow your
heart.' But Nita tried to stop it. Nita couldn't
get over it. Cried. Temper. That's it. Look at
her now. 'Sh! Don't let her see you."

But Anita wasn't looking at me and she wasn't

crying. I suppose Great-aunt must have known
what she was talking about; but it wasn't easy to
imagine my cousin soft and red-eyed like that great,
good-natured Miss Howe. Her little sharp face
looked as controlled as if it were carved. Yet, as
she said herself, she was shaken. That showed in
the jerkiness of her movements, the sharpening of
her voice, in the break-up of her accustomed flow
of words into staccato, like a river that has come
to some rocks : and her hands had a clock-work,
incessant movement, clutch-clutch, fingers on palm,
that her eyes repeated. They were everywhere at
once, resting, flitting, settling again, yet seeing
nothing, I think, while she listened to Mr. Flood
and grew more irritated with every word.

" Why bad news? " said Great-aunt in my ear.
" It's a son, isn't it? "

I hesitated.

" Oh, Auntie, didn't you hear? " (She had heard,
you know. I had seen her shrinking back when
Anita screamed at her, with that dreadful shrinking that you see in an animal threatened by a head-
blow. She had been leaning forward, and eager.
She must have heard.)

" Hear? They all talk," she quavered. " ' Be
quiet,' says Anita. Ah, I've spoilt her. Now
Madala—— What's the time, my dear? Why
don't she come? "

" Auntie—Auntie—— "

" Eh? " she said. " Why don't Madala come? "

"Auntie—you've forgotten. She's been ill."

"Ah—and she'll be worse before she's better," said Great-aunt briskly. "'Sh! Listen to my daughter."

We listened: at least, I listened. Great-aunt cocked her head on one side, still as a bird, for a minute; then, like a bird, she was re-assured and fell to her knitting again.

Anita and Mr. Flood were quarrelling.

"Why shouldn't I? Tell me that! Is anyone better fitted? Who knows as much about her as I do? Didn't I discover her, hacking on two pounds a week? Didn't I recognize what she was? Who sent her to Mitchell and Bent? Who introduced her everywhere? Who bullied her into writing *Ploughed Fields?* Who was the best friend she ever had—even if I didn't make the parade of being fond of her that—— Oh, I've no patience! What would the world know of Madala Grey if it weren't for me?"

"But—oh, of course we all know how good you were to her, Miss Serle, indeed I can guess by what you've done for me——" began the Baxter girl.

Mr. Flood's tongue tip showed between his red lips. I think he would have made some comment but for the hand pressing on his shoulder.

"But——?" said the woman behind the hand.

"I only mean—'genius will out,' won't it?"

"Genius? Big word!" said Miss Howe.

"Not too big." The Baxter girl reddened enthusiastically.

"'Genius will out?' Not Madala Grey's. She didn't know she had any. I don't believe she ever fully realized—— Why, it was the merest chance that *Eden Walls* didn't go into the fire. If it hadn't been for me—if it hadn't been for me——"

"Ah—*you!*" Miss Howe squared up to her. "Now just what (among friends) have you stood to gain? Fond of her? Oh yes, you were, Anita! Don't tell me! But in spite of yourself, eh? But that wasn't what you were after. You didn't get the pleasure out of her that—I did, for instance. You used to exhaust Madala. I've seen you do it. You—you drained her."

"Yes, I did. I meant to," said Anita with her laugh. "Pleasure!"

"And she thought you were fond of her. She used to flare if anyone attacked you. Poor Madala!"

"Poor? Why? I shall give it all back." Anita gave her a long cool look. "I—I hate debts," said Anita.

Miss Howe flushed brightly.

"If you were cursed with the artistic temperament——" She broke off and began again. "If I were a poor devil of a Bohemian in a hole, it's not to you I'd go——"

"—twice!" said Anita.

Again they eyed each other. Miss Howe, still flushing, chose her words.

68

LEGEND

"Madala never lent. That wasn't in her. She gave. Time, money, love—she gave. You took, it was understood, rather than hurt her feelings by refusing. But it was always free gift."

"Not to me." Anita held her head high. "I shall pay. And interest too."

"Oh, the *Life!* Are you really going to attempt a *Life?*" Miss Howe recovered herself with a laugh, while Mr. Flood repeated curiously—

"Yes, but then what were you after, Anita? What do you stand to gain?"

"Reflected glory," came from behind him.

She turned as if she had been stung.

"Reflected? Let her keep it! Reflected? Am I never to have anything of my own? Oh, wait!"

"You can't get much of yourself into a life of Madala Grey though. You've too much sense of style for that," Mr. Flood insisted. "We both hate a biographer who 'I says, says I.'"

"Oh, it shall be all Madala Grey. I promise you that," she said with her thin smile.

"Humph! It's a notion." Miss Howe was really interested, I could see—yet with a flush on her cheek still. "It's your sort of work too, Anita! You're—happier—in critical work."

"Oh, don't hedge. Don't be delicate with me. I can't create, that's what you mean. Do you think that's news to me? Is there a critic who has failed to make it clear to me? I can record— but I can't create. Good! I can't create. I can't do what she did—what you do, Jasper—what even Beryl here does. But——" she paused an instant, " you should be afraid of me for all that. I can pry. Little, nasty, mean word, isn't it? It's me ! "

The Baxter girl laughed uncertainly and then stopped because Anita's eyes were on her.

" I've eyes. I—" she opened and shut her tiny hands before them—" I've claws. I can pry you open, any of you—if I choose. I haven't chosen. You've not been worth while. But—Madala ! " and here she released the uneasy Baxter girl— " Madala's my chance—my chance—my chance ! Madala Grey—look at her—coming into her kingdom at twenty—that babe ! And me ! Look at me ! Do you know what my life has been, any of you ? Oh, you come to my house to meet my lionets, and we're very good friends, and you're afraid of my reviews, and so I have my position, I suppose. But what do you know about me ? When I was fifteen—and it's thirty years ago—I said to myself, ' Now what shall I do with my life ? ' Mother—" she shot her a glance : she didn't even trouble to lower her voice, " she'd have drudged me and dressed me and married me, I suppose, to three hundred a year and the city—oh, with the best of motives. I fought. I fought. That's why I'm an ungrateful daughter. I'm supposed to be, I think. My people were so sorry for my mother. My people thought me a fool. I saw through them. Yes,

70

and I saw through myself. That's the kind of fool I was. Didn't I reckon it out? I hadn't a charm. I hadn't a talent. I had my *will*. That's all I had. I taught myself. Work? You don't know what work means, you ten and five-talented. There's not a book worth reading that I haven't read. There's not the style of a master that I haven't studied, that I couldn't reproduce at a pinch. There's not a man or a woman in London today, worth knowing—from my point of view— that I haven't contrived to know. The people who've arrived—how I've studied them, the ways of them, the methods of them. And what's the end of it all? That—" she jerked her head to the row of her own books on the shelf behind her, " and my column in the *Matins*, and some comforting hundreds a year, and—my knowledge of myself. Oh, I've turned out good work. I know that. I have judgment. That's why I judge myself. I've always been rigid with myself. And so I know when I look at my books—though I can say that they are sounder, better work, in better English, that they have more knowledge behind them, than the books of a dozen of you people who arrive— yet I know that they have failed. People don't read me. People don't want me. Why? I have my name. I've the name of a well-known critic, but—I'm only a name. I'm not alive. The public doesn't touch hands with me. Now why? Oh, how I've tormented myself. Nearly thirty years

71

LEGEND

I've given, of unremitting labour, to my art, to
my career. There's not a thought or a wish that
I haven't sacrificed to it. And then that child of
twenty comes along, without knowledge, without
training, without experience, and gets at one leap,
mark you all, at one leap, more than I've achieved
in thirty years. Some people, I suppose, would
submit. Well, I won't. I wouldn't. Does my
will go for nothing? I *will* have my share. ' Reflected glory,' yes, I've stooped to that. I've
exploited her, if you like to call it that. When
I think of the day I discovered her——" She
paused an instant, dragging her hand wearily over
her eyes—" I was at my zero that day. The
Famous Women had been out a week. The reviews
—oh, the reviews! Respectful, courteous, luke-
warm. If they'd attacked me, if they'd slated,
I'd have rejoiced. But they respect me and they're
bored. They know it's sound work and they're
bored. I bore people. I bore you—all of you.
Do you think I'm blind? That night I read the
manuscript of *Eden Walls*. (Wasn't it kind of me
—it wasn't even typed!) And then I saw my
chance. I saw how far she'd got at twenty, and
I thought—' I'll take my chance. I'll take this
genius. I'll make her fond of me. I'll help her. I'll
worm myself into her. I'll abase myself. I'll toady.
I'll do anything. But I will find out how she does
it. I will find out the secret. I'll find it and I'll
make it my own. I'll serve for her as Jacob served
72

for Rachel; but she shall serve me in the end.'
I have watched. I have studied. I have puzzled.
I believe I've grasped it at last. I know myself
and I know her. If genius is life—the power to
give life—is it that? then I'm barren. I can't
make life as Madala can. But—listen to me!
Listen to me all of you! I can take a living thing
—I can cut it open alive. That's what I shall do
with this life-maker—this easy genius. I've taken
her to pieces, flesh and blood, bone and ligament
and muscle, every secret of her mind and her heart
and her soul. The life, the *real* life of Madala Grey,
the rise and fall of a genius, that's what I'm going
to make plain. She's been a puzzle to you all,
with her gifts and her ways and her crazy marriage
—she's not a mystery to me. I tell you I've got
her, naked, pinned down, and now I shall make
her again. Isn't it fair? She ought to thank me.
' Dead,' he says. Who's to blame? She chose to
kill herself. What right had she to take risks? I—
I've refrained. She couldn't. She threw away her
lamp. But I—I take it. I light it again. Finding's
keeping. It's mine."

Her voice ripped on the high note like a rag on
a nail, and she checked, panting. Her hand went
up to her throat as the fumy air rasped it.

" Mine ! " she cried again, coughing. There was
wild-fire in her eyes as she challenged them.

The little space between her solitariness and their
grouped attention was filled with fog and silence

and lamp-light, woven as it were into a fifth element. It was like a pool to be crossed. And across it, in answer, a laugh rippled out.

I don't know who it was that laughed. I did not recognize the voice. Sometimes, looking back, I think it was the laugh of their collective soul.

"Oh!" cried Anita, and stopped as if she had been awakened suddenly by a blow—as if the little wondering, wincing cry had been struck out of her by a blow on the face. She stood thus a moment, uncertain. Then she too laughed, nervously, apologetically.

"One talks," she said, "among friends."

Miss Howe made a wry face.

"Lord, we're a queer set of friends! How we love one another!"

"You've all of you been awfully good to me," said the Baxter girl. But her gratitude was too general to be acceptable. Even I could have told her that.

"Oh, we do our best for you," said Mr. Flood.

She looked at him from under her lashes.

"Yes, and she's thinking this minute what a nice little scene this would make for her new book —touched up, of course," said the woman behind him.

"Art — selection — Jimmy Whistler——" Mr. Flood was one indistinct murmur.

"With herself her own heroine again, eh?" Miss Howe baited her.

LEGEND

" I didn't.   I wasn't."

" Better folk than you do it, child !   Anita says so.   Don't they, Anita ? "

" Oh," said Anita heavily, " I wish Madala Grey were here.   I wish she hadn't died.   If she were here she wouldn't—you'd never—she wouldn't let you laugh at me."

Miss Howe looked at her intently.   There was a quick little run of expression across her large handsome face, like a hand playing a scale.   It showed, that easily moved, easily read face, surprise, interest, concern, and, in the end, the sentimental impulse of your kind fur-clad woman to the beggar on the curb.   ' Why !   I believe she's cold !   I don't like it !   Give her tuppence, quick ! '   She was out of her chair, overwhelming Anita, in one impetuous heave of drapery.

" You're right, Nita !   We're pigs !   Something's wrong with us.   'Pologize.   You know we don't mean it."

Anita endured her right-and-left kisses.

" You do mean it," was all she said.

She was shrunk to such a small grey creature again.   I thought to myself—' Fire ?   It's not even diamond-sparkle.   She's as dull as stone.'

Miss Howe was eagerly remorseful.

" We don't.   I don't know what's got into us tonight.   It's the fog.   There's something evil about a fog.   Distorting.   It yellows over one's soul."

" It isn't only tonight," said the Baxter girl,

with her sidelong, ' can-I-risk-it? ' look at them.
" The fog's been coming on for months."

" And you mean——? " The blonde lady never
snubbed the Baxter girl. It struck me suddenly,
as their eyes met, that there was the beginning of
a likeness between them. The Baxter girl at fifty
—with dyed hair——? But it was only an idea
of mine. I'm always seeing imaginary likenesses.
I remember that those Academy pictures of Kent
Rehan's always set me to work wondering—' That
woman with the face turned away—I've seen her
somewhere—of whom does she remind me?—where
have I seen her? ' And yet, of course, in those
days I knew nothing of Madala Grey.

But the Baxter girl was answering—

" It—it's cheek, I know, but it's true. When I
first came—" then, with a swift propitiatory glance
at Anita—" when you first let me come—the Nights
weren't like this. You weren't like this any of
you——"

" Upon—my—word ! " said Miss Howe with her
benevolent chuckle. " Nita ! Listen to the infant ! "

" Like what ? " Mr. Flood moved uneasily.

The Baxter girl turned to him enthusiastically.

" Oh, I used to think you such wonderful
people——"

" Did you now? " Miss Howe teased her.

" Let be ! let be ! " said Mr. Flood impatiently.
" Well, dear lady ? "

" Oh, I did ! I'd read all your stuff. I believe

76

I could write out *The Orchid House* from memory still."

His eyes lit up as he challenged her—

> "'Sour!' said the fox at her feet,
> 'How can she ripen windy-high?
> Sour!' said the fox with his nose to the sky—"

He was as pleased as a child with a toy when she capped it—

> "Then a grape dropped off. It was rotten sweet.

There!" she flushed at him triumphantly. And then—"Now did you mean——? Who was in your mind? Were they anyone we know? I've always wanted to ask you."

But before he could answer her the blonde lady leaned forward and whispered in his ear. He turned to her with a glance of interest and amusement, but with his lips still moving and his mind still running on an answer to the Baxter girl. The blonde lady whispered again, and then he turned right round to answer her, shelving his arms on her knees. I couldn't hear what they said, but it was just as if she had beckoned him into another room. He was withdrawn from the conversation and from the Baxter girl for as long as that blonde lady chose.

Miss Howe looked at them with her broad smile.

" Tell us, Beryl! We're listening, anyhow!" she said invitingly.

But the Baxter girl's chin went up. The touch of annoyance in her voice made it twang, made her commonness suddenly noticeable. She was bearable when she was in awe of them, but now she was asserting herself, and that meant that she was inclined to be noisy.

"Oh, my opinion doesn't count, of course! But—" she swung like a pendulum between her two manners—" oh, I *did* enjoy myself at first. It was the way you all talked. You knew everyone. You'd read everything. You frothed adventures. Like champagne it was, meeting all the people. I used to write my head off, the week after. And you were all kind to me from the first. I suppose it was Madala. She never let one feel out of it. But I thought it was all of you. I had the feeling —' the gods *aren't* jealous gods.' But now it's—" she looked at them pertly, " it's fog on Olympus."

" You needn't—honour us, you know, Beryl," said Anita sharply.

She answered with her furtive look.

" I know. And I don't think—I don't want to come as much as I did."

" In that case——" Anita ruffled up.

" Fog! Fog!" cried Miss Howe clapping her hands. And then—" All the same, Nita, people are dropping off. The Whitneys haven't been for weeks. When did Roy Huth come last? And the Golding crowd? I marvel that *he* turns up still." She nodded towards Kent Rehan. " Oh, you know,

78

we're like a row of beads when the string's been
pulled out. We lie in a line for a time, but a touch
will send us rolling in all directions."

" Yes," said the Baxter girl vehemently, " the
heart's out of it somehow. I'm not ungrateful. It's
just because I used to love coming so."

Miss Howe looked down at Anita, not unkindly.

" Give it up, Nita ! The Nights have served their
turn. It sounds ungracious, but things have to end
sometime or other. Hasn't the time come? Hasn't
it come tonight? "

" But you've been coming all this year just the
same," said Anita stubbornly.

Miss Howe shrugged her shoulders. It was the
Baxter girl who answered—

" Ah, but there was always just a chance of
seeing Madala."

At that Anita, who had been sitting as steely
stiff as a needle in a pin-cushion, got up, shaking off
Miss Howe's persuasive, detaining hand and the
overflow of her skirts. The cushions tumbled after
her on to the floor.

" As to that," she said, " and don't imagine that I
haven't known what you came for, all of you——"

" Eh ? "

Her voice was sharp enough to have recalled any
one and it recalled Mr. Flood. He returned to the
conversation with the air of dragging the blonde lady
after him. She had the manner of one hanging
back and protesting, and laughing still over some

LEGEND

secret understanding. " Eh? " said he. " What's
that about Madala? "

Anita looked from one to another.

" I'm telling you," she said. " I've told you
already, I can give you Madala Grey. Come here
and I'll give you Madala Grey still. That's what
you want, isn't it, to be amused? She amused
you."

" She did, bless her! " said Miss Howe.

" It was her brains," said the Baxter girl.

" A beautiful creature," said Mr. Flood slowly.

" Not she! " The lady behind him was smiling.
" She made you think so. She made men think
so. But how? That intrigued me. Oh, she was
prettyish : but that was all. I used to watch
her——"

" Envy? " said he.

" No, not envy," said that woman slowly. " She
was too—innocent—how could one envy? She
didn't know her own strength. She said—' Don't
hurt me,' with a sword at her side."

" Excalibur." It came from Mr. Flood. " Magic."

" No, Madala—just Madala." Miss Howe sighed.
" It's no good, Anita, you can't give us back
Madala."

But my cousin, looking at them, laughed in her
turn.

" Madala? You fools! You've never had her.
But you shall! Oh, wait! My books are dull,
aren't they? Yet you'll be here, you know, every

80

month, thick as bees, to listen to me. A chapter a month, that's all I'll give to you. *I* don't write three novels a year. But you'll come, you'll come. Proof? There's plenty of proof. See here."

She went swiftly across to the outer room. There was a large carved desk standing on the little table by the window. She picked it up. It was too big for her. It filled her arms so that she staggered under the weight.

" Oh, Kent ! " she called.

He came back to the foggy room with a visible wrench.

" Here, that's too heavy for you. Let me." He took it from her.

" The table—here. Thank-you, oh, thank-you, Kent." She veiled her voice as she spoke to him. " It's heavy—it's so full—books—papers——"

He put it down for her and nodded, and was straying away again when she stopped him.

" Kent ! Don't sit by yourself. We—" her voice was for him alone—" we're talking about—her. I was going to show them—Kent, stay here with us."

He waited while she talked to him. And she talked very sweetly and kindly. She was the quiet, chiffony little creature again with the pretty, pure voice. *I* couldn't make her out. She looked up at him and said something too low for me to catch, and then—

" There's your chair. Isn't that always your

chair?" And so left him and turned to the table and the box and the others.

But he did not take the saddle-bag near Anita's own seat. He looked irresolutely from one to another of the group that watched Anita fumbling with her keys. He looked, and his face softened, at Great-aunt, muttering over her needles. He looked at the empty chair beside me. He looked at me and found me watching him. Then, as I smiled at him just a little, he came to me and sat down. But he said nothing to me, and so I was quiet too.

But Anita was busy, hands and eyes and tongue all busy.

" When she married, you know, in that hole and corner fashion——" Then, as if in answer, though nobody had spoken—" Well, what else was it, when nobody knew? when even I didn't know——"

There was a movement in the chair beside me, and turning, I caught the ending of a glance towards my cousin. A new look, I found it, on that passive face, a roused and wondering and scornful look that transformed it. But, even as I caught it, it faded again to that other look of bleak indifference, a look to know and dread on any creature's face, a look that must not stay on any fellow-creature's face. I knew that well enough. So I said the first words that came, in my lowest voice, lest they should hear.

But they were talking. They did not hear.

LEGEND

" I'm sure that Great-aunt knew.' Indeed I
thought so. I think that Great-aunt would always
be kind and guessing with a girl. Then I wondered
at myself for daring it and thought nervously—
' He'll snub me. He'll be right to snub me——'
But he looked across at Great-aunt kindly and
said, in just such a withdrawn voice as mine—
" Yes, of course, if ever there was a time when——"
Then he half smiled. " Poor old lady ! But she's
changed. She used to be so brisk and managing,
more like fifty than seventy. But this year's aged
her. She wanted, you know, to give some pearls—
her own pearls. But pearls spell sorrow. And Anita
would have objected. She told me all about it."
" She was speaking of them tonight." We both
turned again and looked at her. She had dropped
her knitting, or it had slipped from her knee, and
she sat in her chair staring down at it with a terrible,
comical air of helplessness. Then she caught his
eye and forgot the knitting and nodded at him.
" I think—" I said, " I don't think she understands. She asked me—she forgets I'm a stranger.
She asked me——" I broke off. I couldn't say
to him—' She asked me about Miss Grey and she
doesn't realize that she's dead.' One's afraid of
the brutality of words. But he understood. There
was a simplicity about him that re-assured one.
And he never said—' It's Anita's business. It's not
your business,' as anyone else might have done.
He just said, once again—

" Poor old lady ! " and hesitated a minute. Then he got up and went across to her and picked up her wools. I don't think the others noticed him go. Anita didn't. She was talking too fast.

" —left a trunk-full of papers and so on. I'd often stored boxes for her. Somehow it never got sent down. I came across it only yesterday. I thought to myself that there was no harm in putting things straight. You know I'm literary executor? Oh yes. She said to me soon after her marriage, half in joke, that she supposed she had got to make a will—and what about her MSS.? ' I can't have *him* worried.' I offered at once. You see I know so exactly her attitude in literature. There's a good deal of unpublished stuff—early stuff. But all in hopeless confusion. Tumbled up with bills and programmes and one or two drafts of letters— or so I imagine. She had that annoying habit— that ugly modern habit—of beginning without any invocation, and never a date. But there's one letter—there's the draft of a letter that's important from my point of view." She broke off with a half laugh. " It sounds a ridiculous statement to make about Madala Grey of all people, but do you know that she couldn't express herself at all easily on paper? "

Miss Howe nodded.

" Do I know? I've known her re-write a letter half a dozen times before she got it to her liking—

84

no, not business letters, letters to her intimates.
A most comical trick. Scribble, scribble, scribble—
slash! and then crunch goes the sheet into a ball,
into the grate, or near it, till it looked as if she
were playing snow-balls, and then Madala begins
again—and again—and again. Yet she talked well.
She talked easily."

" Isn't that in keeping?" Mr. Flood struck in.
" She didn't express so much herself in her speech
as the mood of the moment."

" As the mood of the companion of the moment
more likely," the blonde lady corrected.

He nodded agreement.

" But for herself—go to her books."

" Or her letters—her careful, conscientious letters.
But she was careless about her drafts," said Anita
significantly.

Mr. Flood looked at her curiously.

" What's up that sleeve of yours, Anita?"

She was quick.

" You shall read it, in its place. But the trouble
is——" She hesitated. She gave the little nervous
cough that always ushered in her public lectures.
" We've all written books," she said, " all except
you, Blanche——"

The blonde lady blinked her sleepy eyes.

" You're all so strenuous," she purred. " I love
to watch you being strenuous. So soothing."

" Well, I was going to say, it's easy enough to
end a book, but have you ever got to the beginning?

I never have. One steps backward, and backward
again——"

"I know," cried the Baxter girl. "Till you get
tired of it at last and begin writing from where you
are, but you never really get your foot on the
starting-point, on the spring-board, as you might
say."

"That's it. Yes, Jasper, I've got material up
my sleeve, but frankly, I don't know how to place
it. I don't know where to begin. The facts of
her life, her conversation, her literary work, her
letters—I go on adding to my material till I am
overwhelmed with all that I have got to say about
her. But I don't want to begin with facts. Facts
are well enough, but think how one can twist them!
I want the woman behind the facts. I want the
answer to the question that is the cause of a
biography such as mine is to be—the question—
'What was Madala Grey?' Not who, mark you,
but further back, deeper into herself—'*What* was
Madala Grey?'"

"Why, a genius," said the Baxter girl glibly.

Anita neither assented nor dissented.

"Ah—" she said frowning, "but that's not
the beginning either. At once we take our step
backward again—'What is genius?'"

"Isn't talent good enough?" said Mr. Flood
acidly.

"But does one mean talent?" She was still
frowning. "Everyone's got talent. I'm sick of

talent. But she—she mayn't be a great one—how she'd have laughed at being called a great one!—but she makes her dolls live. And isn't that the blood-link between the greatest gods and the littlest gods? Life-givers? Life-makers? Oh, I only speak for myself; but she made her book-world real to me, therefore for me she had genius. Whether or not I convince you is the test of whether my life-work, my *Life* of her—fails or succeeds."

" I suppose you wouldn't trust it to Madala?" said Miss Howe softly.

" Trust what?"

" To convince us."

She answered, suspicious rather than comprehending, for indeed Miss Howe's tone was very smooth—

" What do you mean? *I'*m writing her life."

Miss Howe was inscrutable.

" Of course you are. Fire ahead. Genius, wasn't it?"

Anita shrugged her shoulders.

" What's in a name? It's the quality itself that fascinates me. I want to account for it. I want to trace it to its source. Worth doing, isn't it? But do you realize the difficulties? Sometimes I feel hopeless. I've known her five years, and her books I know by heart, and I'm only just beginning to decide whether to call her a romantic or a realist."

" A realist. Look at *Eden Walls*," said the Baxter girl.

LEGEND

" A romantic. Look at *The Resting-place*," said Miss Howe.

Mr. Flood over-rode them.

" Dear ladies, you confuse the terms. It amazes me how people always confuse the terms. Your so-called realist, your writer who depicts what we call reality, the outward life, that is, of flesh and dirt and misery—don't you see that he is in truth a romantic—a man (or woman) who lives in a fair world of his own, a paradise of the imagination? Out of that secure world of his he peers curiously at ours, and writes of it as we dare not write, writes down every sordid, garish, tragi-comic detail. Your so-called realist can afford the humour of Rabelais, the horror of Dostoievsky, the cheerful flesh and blood of Fielding. Why shouldn't he be truthful? It's not his world. Don't you see? But your so-called romantic, he lives in this real world. He knows it so well that he has to shut his eyes or he would die of its reality. So he escapes into the world of romance, the world of beauty within his own mind—nowhere but in his own mind. Who is our dreamer of dreams? Shelley, the realist! Blake jogged elbows with poverty and squalor all his life, and he was the prophet and the king of all spirits. Don't you see? And Goethe—the biographers will tell you that Goethe began as a realist and ended as a romantic. I say it was the other way round. What did he know of reality in the twenties? Its discovery was the romantic

adventure of his young genius. But when he was
old and worldly and wise—then he wrote his
romances, to escape from his own knowledge. Oh,
I tell you, you should turn the words round. Now
take Shakespeare——"

"It's not fair to take Shakespeare," said Miss
Howe. "It's the Elephant and the Crawfishes
over again. Let's keep to the crawfishes! Let's
keep to our own generation!"

"Well, if I were Anita I should begin by showing
Madala as a romantic—as the young romantic pro-
ducing the most startlingly realistic book we've had
for a decade. Indeed to me, you know, her development is marked by her books in the sharpest way.
It's the young, the curious, the observant Madala
in *Eden Walls*. The whole book is a shout of discovery, of young, horrified discovery, of the ugliness
of life. It's as if she said—'Listen! Listen!
These things actually happen to some people. Isn't
it awful?' She dwells on it. She insists on every
detail. She can't get away from it. And yet she
can hardly believe it, that young Madala. But in
Ploughed Fields already the tone's changing. It's
a pleasanter book, a more sophisticated book. It
interests profoundly, but it's careful not to upset
one—an advance, of course. Yet I, you know, hear
our Madala's voice in it still, an uneasy voice—
'Hush! Hush! These things happen to most
people. Pretend not to notice.' And in the last
book, in the pretty, impossible romance, there you

have your realist full-fledged—'Shut your eyes! Come away quickly! These things are happening to *me!*'" He leant back again folding his arms and dropping his chin. And then, because Miss Howe was looking at him as if she were amused—"I tell you I know. I recognize the symptoms. I'm a realist myself. That's why I write romantic poetry. Have to. It's that or drugs. How else shall one get through life?"

"Jasper!" said the blonde lady. But for once he didn't turn to her. He shrugged his shoulders.

"Don't worry. Who'll believe me?"

The Baxter girl was breathless.

"Oh, but I do. It's a new Madala, of course. But I believe it explains her."

"But the facts of her life don't agree," began Miss Howe.

"Ah, Anita's got to make 'em," said Mr. Flood languidly. "Isn't that the art of biography?"

But Anita was deadly serious.

"You don't begin far enough back. My springboard is not—what is Madala? but—what is genius? How does it happen? Is it immaculate birth? or is it begotten of accident upon environment? That is to say—is it inspiration or is it experience? I speak of the divine fire, you understand, not of the capacity for resolving it into words or paint or stone. That's craft, a very different thing. You say that Madala was not a genius in the big sense—yes, I'll admit that even, for the argument's sake—

but even you will concede her the beginnings of it. So my difficulty is just the same. I've never believed in instinctive genius. Yet how can she, at twenty, have had the experience (that she had the craft is amazing enough) to cope with *Eden Walls?* Romantic curiosity isn't enough explanation, Jasper! Look at her certainty of touch. Look at her detail. Look how she gets inside that woman's mind. That's the fascination of it. It's such a document. Now how does she know it? That's what intrigues me. Madala and a street woman! Where's the connection? How does she get inside her? Because she does get inside her."

" Oh, it's real enough," said the blonde lady.

" It must be. You should have seen the letters she received ! Amazing, some of them."

" Anita, they amazed *her*. I remember her getting one while she was staying with us. She looked thoroughly frightened. She said—' But Lila, I didn't realize—it was just a story. But this poor thing, she says it's true ! She says it's happened to her ! What are we to do ? ' You know, she was nearly crying. It was some hysterical woman who had read the book. But Madala always believed in people. I know she wrote to her. I believe she helped her. But she never told you much about her doings."

" Oh, her sentimental side doesn't interest me. What I ask myself is—how does she know, as she

obviously does know, all that her wretched drab
of a heroine thought and felt and suffered? "

" Instinct! Imagination! " said the Baxter girl.
" It must be the explanation."

" It isn't. It isn't. Oh, I've puzzled it out.
I'm convinced that from the beginning it's experience. Don't flare, Lila, I don't mean literal
experience. Not in *Eden Walls*, anyhow. Later,
of course—but we're discussing *Eden Walls*. Imagination, do you say, Beryl? But the imagination
must have a fact for its root. I'll grant you that
imagination is so essentially a quality of youth that
the merest rootlet of a reality is enough to set a
young artist beanstalk climbing. But the older he
grows, the wiser, the more versed in reality, the
less he trusts his imagination, the more, in conse-
quence, his imagination flags and withers; till he
ends—one sees it happen again and again—as the
recorder merely of his own actual experiences and
emotions. It's only the greatest who escape that
decay of the imagination. Do you think that
Madala did? Look at *Eden Walls*. Remember
what we know about her. Can't you see that the
skeleton of *Eden Walls* is Madala's own life? Consider her history. She leaves what seems to have
been a happy childhood behind her and sets out
on adventure—very young. So does the woman
in *Eden Walls*. The parallel's exact. Madala's
Westering Hill and the *Breckonridge* of the novel
are the same place. The house, the lane, the

country-side, she doesn't trouble to disguise them.
Again—Madala's adventure is ushered in by
calamity: and tragedy—(you can see the artist
transmuting the mere physical calamity into
tragedy) tragedy happens to the woman in *Eden
Walls*. Remember how much more Madala dwelt
on the sense of loneliness and lovelessness, on the
anguish of the loss of something to love her, than
on what one might call the—er—official emotions
of a betrayed woman. Didn't it strike you?
Doesn't that show that she was depending on her
experience rather than on her imagination, fitting
her own private grief to an imaginary case? Then,
in America, she has the struggle for meat and drink,
for mere existence. So does the woman in *Eden
Walls*. Madala does not go under. The woman
in *Eden Walls* does. It's the first real difference.
But I maintain that in reality the parallel still
continues, that, in imagination, Madala did go
under over and over again: that she had ever in
front of her the 'suppose, suppose,' that, in drawing
the woman in *Eden Walls*, she is saying to herself—
'Here, but for the grace of God, go I.' And then,
you know, when you think of her, hating that big
city, saving up her pennies, and coming home at
last in a passion of homesickness (if it was home-
sickness—sickness anyhow), can't you see how it
makes her write of that other woman? It's the
gift, the genius, stirring in her: born, not immacu-
lately, but of her own literal experience. Jasper's

right—you can always make facts fit if you think them out : and because I possess that underlying shadow-work (I admit it's no more) of fact to guide me in deciphering her method in the first book, therefore, in the second book and the third book, I find it safe to *deduce* facts to cover the stories, even when I don't possess them. I consider that I'm justified, that *Eden Walls* justifies me. Don't you ? "

" It's plausible," said Mr. Flood thoughtfully.

" Oh, it's convincing," said the Baxter girl reverently. " I feel I've never known Madala Grey before. What it will be when you get it into shape, Miss Serle——"

" In fact," said Miss Howe, " there's only one drawback——"

" And that ? " said Anita swiftly.

" Only Madala's own account."

" She never discussed her methods," said Anita sharply.

" Just so ! You're not the only person who's— pumped. I remember seeing her once surrounded, in her lion days. I remember her ingenuous explanations. She did her best to oblige them— ' Honestly, I don't know. One just sits down and imagines.' And then—' That's quite easy. But it's awfully difficult writing it down.' That's the explanation, Nita. A deliberate, even unconscious self-exploitation is all nonsense. Madala's not clever enough."

LEGEND

" Not clever enough ! "

" No. You're much cleverer than she was. You have twice her brains. You can't think, Anita, what brains you've got. You've got far too many to understand a simple person. I don't agree, you know, with ' genius.' I can't throw a word like that about so lightly. But as far as it went with Madala, it was the same sort of genius that makes a crocus push in the spring. Your theory—oh, it's plausible, as Jasper says, but don't you see that it destroys all the charm of her work ? It's the innocence of her knowledge, the simplicity of her attitude to her own insight that to me is moving. She touches pitch, yet her fingers are clean. It's her view of her story that arrests one, not her story, not her facts, not her mere plot."

" No, the plot is conventional, I'll grant you that. She was always content with old bottles."

" Yes, and when the new wine burst them and made a mess on the carpet, Madala was always so surprised and indignant."

Mr. Flood giggled.

" Pained is the word, dear lady—surprised and pained. Do you remember when *Eden Walls* was banned ? "

" I don't suppose she talked to you about it, Jasper," said Miss Howe sharply.

" I ? I was never of her counsels. But I got my amusement out of the affair. Dear, delightful woman ! She behaved like a schoolgirl sent to

Coventry. I remember congratulating her on the advertisement, and she would hardly speak to me. But it suited her, the blush."

"*Wasn't* it an advertisement!" said the Baxter girl longingly.

"If one could have got her to see it," said Anita. "But no, she insisted on being ashamed of herself. She said to me once that the critics had 'read in' things that she had never dreamed of—that it made her doubt her own motives—that she felt dirtied and miserable. And yet she wouldn't alter one of those scenes. Obstinate! She could be very obstinate."

"Oh, which scenes?" The Baxter girl stuck her elbows on the table and her chin in her fists. Her eyes sparkled. "Oh, then, Miss Serle, did you—? did she come to you in the early days? Did you help her too?"

"My daughter—very kind to young people!"

It was a mere mutter, but I recognized the swing of the phrase. Anita didn't. She was busy with the Baxter girl.

"I don't say that there would be no Madala Grey today if I——"

"*But*——" said Mr. Flood.

"*But*—" said Miss Howe, "she's Anita's discovery. We're never to forget that, are we, darling?"

"Oh, I knew that," said the Baxter girl, trying to be tactful. "But *Eden Walls* was written before you knew her, wasn't it? I understood—I didn't

know, I mean," she explained to them, "that Miss
Serle had—blue-pencilled——"

"I did and I didn't." Anita laughed, as if in
spite of herself. "I confess I thought at the time
that it needed revision. Mind you, I never questioned the quality, but I knew what the public
would stand and what it wouldn't. Of course, I
didn't want the essentials altered. But there were
certain cuts—— However, nothing would move
her."

"That's funny. She never gave me the impression that she believed in herself so strongly."

"Oh, her *pose* was diffidence," said the blonde
lady.

"But she didn't believe in herself. It was
obvious. When I went through her MS. and blue-
pencilled, she was most grateful. She agreed to
everything and took the MS. away to remodel."

"And then?"

"I heard nothing more of her—for weeks. Finally
I wrote and asked her to come and see me. She
came. She was delightful. I had told her, you
know, about the *Anthology* the first time I met
her. I remember that I was annoyed with myself
afterwards. I'm not often indiscreet. But she
had a—a knack—a way with her. I hardly know
how to describe it."

"One told her things," said the Baxter girl.

"Just so. One told her things. And she had
brought me a mass of material—some charming

LEGEND

American verse (you remember? in the last section but one) that I had never come across. She had been reading for me at the British Museum in her spare time. I confess I was touched. We talked, I remember——" She sighed reminiscently. " It was not until she made a move to go that I recollected myself. ' Well,' I said, ' and how about *Eden Walls?* ' She fidgeted. She looked thoroughly guilty. At last it came out. She hadn't altered a line. She had tried her utmost. She had drafted and re-drafted. She had finally given it up in despair and just got work in some obscure newspaper office—' a most absorbing office!' But there—you know Madala when she's interested—was interested——"

" Don't," said Miss Howe softly.

But Anita went on—

" ' Well but—' I said to her—' that's all very well. But you're not going to abandon *Eden Walls*, are you?' Then it all came out. Yes, she was. She knew I was right. She wasn't conceited. She quite saw that the book was useless. It just meant that she couldn't write novels and that she mustn't waste any more time. ' But my dear Miss Grey,' I said, ' you mean to say that you'd rather leave the book unpublished than alter a couple of chapters, remodel a couple of characters?' ' But I can't,' she said, ' I can't. They happened that way.' ' Then make them happen differently,' I said. But no, she couldn't. ' Oh well,' I said at last—'if you're so absolutely sure of yourself, if you're prepared to set up your judgment——' That distressed her. I can hear her now. 'But I don't set up my judgment. I'll burn the wretched stuff to-morrow if you say it's trash. I knew it would be, in my heart. But— I can't alter it, because—because it happened that way.' Then I had an idea. 'To you?' I said. She looked at me. She laughed. She said—'Miss Serle, you've written ten books to my one. Don't pretend you don't know how a story happens.'" Anita nodded at us. "You see? Evasive. I think it was from that moment that I began to have my theory of her."

"Well — and what next?" demanded Miss Howe.

"She would have said good-bye if I had let her. I stopped her. 'Reconsider it,' I said. She beamed at me, chastened but quite cheerful. 'Oh, I'll try another some day,' she said. 'I suppose I'm not old enough. I was a fool to think I could.' At that, of course, I gave in. I wasn't going to lose sight of *Eden Walls*. I told her to bring it as it was and I'd see what I could do. As you know, Mitchell and Bent jumped at it."

"But it was banned," said the Baxter girl.

"Yes, but everybody read it. You can get it anywhere now. And I can say now—'Thank the gods she didn't touch it.'"

"Then she was right?"

99

"Of course she was right. I knew it all the time."

"And she didn't?"

"Of course she didn't. Mine was critical knowledge. Hers the mere instinct of—whatever you choose to call it. I was afraid of the critics. She didn't know enough to be afraid."

"There's something big about you, Anita!" said Miss Howe suddenly.

Mr. Flood gave the oblique flicker of eyes and mouth that was his smile.

"Yes," he said slowly, "it fits her quite well."

"What?" said Anita sharply.

"The mantle, dear lady."

She shrugged her shoulders.

"Ah—*Gentle dullness ever loves a joke*. What, Beryl?"

"I don't see," the Baxter girl had harked back, "how you can call a book that has been banned conventional."

"Only the plot——"

"Ah, that plot!" Nobody could snub Mr. Flood. "Think, dear lady! Village maiden—faithless lover—lights o' London—unfortunate female—what more do you want?"

"Of course." Anita resumed the reins. "It's as old as *The Vicar of Wakefield*."

"Oh, *that!*" The Baxter girl looked interested. "Do you know, I've never seen it. One of Irving's shows, wasn't it?"

LEGEND

I laughed. I couldn't help it. But they were all quite solemn, even Anita. But then she never did listen to the Baxter girl. She had talked straight through her sentences.

"But it's not the material. It's the way it's handled. It's never been done quite so thoroughly, from the woman's point of view—so unadornedly. People are afraid of their '*poor girls*.' There's a formula that even the Immortals follow. They are all young and beautiful, and they all die. They must. They wouldn't be tragic in continuation. But Madala's woman doesn't. That's the point. There's no pretence at making her a heroine. She's just the ordinary stupidish sheep of a creature, 'gone wrong.' There's no romantic halo, no love-glamour, no pity and terror, just the chronicle of a sordid life. And yet you can't put the book down. At least I couldn't put it down.

"Do *you* like it?" I said to Kent Rehan, as he paused beside me in his eternal pacing from room to room.

He looked at me oddly.

"I respect it," he said. "I don't like it. People misjudged——"

"If it had been the recognized love story"— Mr. Flood's high voice silenced him—"the regularized irregularity, so to speak, it wouldn't have been banned. It was the absence of a love story that the British public couldn't forgive. It was cheated. It was shocked."

101

LEGEND

"But there is a love story at the beginning, isn't there?" I said. "I haven't read far."

Instantly the Baxter girl exhibited me—

"Yes, imagine! She hasn't read it!"

"I've read *The Vicar of Wakefield*," I said. And then I was annoyed that I had shown I was annoyed. But at once Miss Howe helped me. Miss Howe was always nice to me.

"How far have you got? Where the man tires of her? Ah, yes! Well, after that it's just her struggle. She—she earns her living—in the inevitable way. She grows into a miser. She hoards."

Mr. Flood looked acute.

"That's what upset them. They don't mind a Magdalen; but Magdalen unaware, unrepentant, Magdalen preserving her ill-gotten gains—no, that's not quite nice."

"Well, I don't know," said Miss Howe. "If anyone can't feel the spirit it's written in, the passion of pity—I think it's the most pitiful thing I've ever read. It made me shiver. That wretched creature, saving and sparing——" And then to me, for I suppose I showed I was interested— "She wants to get away, you know, to get back into the country. It's her dream. The home-sickness——"

"I suppose such a woman could——?" said the Baxter girl.

"I used to argue it with Madala. Madala always

102

said that, with some people, that animal craving for some special place was like love—a passion that could waste you. She said that every woman must have some devouring passion, for a man, or a child, or a place—*every* woman. And that for a beaten creature like that, it would be *place*—the homing instinct of a cat or a bird. And mixed up with it, religion—the vague shadowy ideal of peace and cleanly beauty—all that the wretched creature tries to express in her phrase—'getting out and living quiet'—that Madala typifies in the word 'Eden.' It meant much to Madala. Don't you remember that passage towards the end of the book where she meets the man, the first man, and brings him home with her—and he doesn't even recognize her, and she doesn't even care?" She picked up a bundle of tattered proofs and turned them over. "Where is it? What an appalling hand she had!" She stood a moment, reading a page and pursing her lips. "Oh, well, what's the use of reading it? We all know it." She flung it down.

"Let me see," I said to the Baxter girl. She drew it towards me. It was the first proof I'd ever seen. It was corrected till it was difficult to read. But I made it out at last.

With the closing of the door she dismissed him with one phrase for ever from her mind—
"And that's that!"

LEGEND

She had long been accustomed thus to summarize her clients, dispassionately, as one classes beasts at a show; and she judged them, not by their clothing or their speech, not by the dark endured hours of their love or by the ticklish after-moment of the reckoning, but rather, as she hovered at the door with her provocative night smile dulled to a business friendliness, by their manner of leaving her.

Always there was the fever to be gone; but some went furtively, with cautious, tiptoe feet that set the stairs a-squeak with mockery. Her smile did not change for the swaggerer who stayed long and took his luck-kiss twice, but her eyes would harden. Mean, cheating mean, to kiss again and never pay again! And some she watched and smiled upon who left her in a brutal silence. For them she had no resentment, rather the sullenness beneath her smile reached out to the revulsion of their bearing as to something welcomed and akin. And some gave back her smile with kindly words—and those she hated.

But when, after his manner, the man had gone, she had, as always, her ritual

She locked her easy door and pulling out the key, put it before her on the table at the bedside. Left and right of it she laid her money down, adding to the night's gains the meagre leavings of her purse. Left and right the little piles grew, one heaped high for the needs of her day and her night, for food and roof and livery, and one a thin scatter of coppers and small silver that took long weeks to change into the dear, the exquisite, the Eden-opening gold. It was the bigger pile that she thrust so carelessly back into her bag, and the scattered ha'pence that she warmed in the cup of her two hands, holding them, jingle-jingle, at her ears, dropping them to her lap again to count anew, piling them before her to a little, narrowing tower, before she

104

opened the child's jewel-case beside her, and, lifting the sheaf of letters that she never read but kept still and would always keep, for the savage pain they gave her when her eyes saw them and her fingers touched them, she poured out the new treasure upon the sacred hoard beneath.

Tenpence saved—and yesterday a shilling! Five shillings last week. Fifty pounds! She would soon have fifty pounds!

She put away the box of money, and so, surrendering at last to the awful bodily fatigue, lay down again upon the tousled bed, not to sleep—her sleeping time was later in the day—but to shut her eyes.

For, by the amazing pity of God, a secret that is not every man's, was hers—the secret of the refuge appointed, behind shut eyes, of the return into eternity that is the shutting down of lids upon the eyes. The window glare, the screaming street below, the blank soiled ceiling with the flies, the walls, the unending pattern of the hateful walls, the clock, the finery, the beastly scents, the loathed familiars of stuff and wood and brass that blinked and creaked at her like voices crying—" Misery ! misery ! misery ! "—these were her world. Yet not her only world. She, who was so dim and blunted a woman-thing, could pass, with the warm dark velvet touch of dropping lids, not into the nullity of sleep, but into the grey place, limitless, timeless, where consciousness knows nothing of the flesh.

She shut her eyes with the sigh of a tired dog, and instantly her soul lay back and floated, resting.

There was no time, no thought, no feeling. There was peace—quiet—greyness. At unmeasured intervals realization washed over her like waves, waves of peace—quiet—greyness. Greyness—she worshipped the blessed greyness. She wanted to give it a beloved name and

105

knew none. ' When I am dead ! —' For ever and ever,
Amen ! '—So she came nearest to ' Eternity.'

Peace—quiet—greyness : greyness enduring for ever,
that could yet be rent asunder like a temple veil and
let in misery—the window glare, the reeking room, the
clodding footsteps, the fingers tapping at her door—a
frail eternity whose walls were slips of flesh.

She called harshly—

" Get out ! Get away ! Put it down outside then,
can't you ? "

There was a mutter and the clank of a scuttle-lid,
and a thud. The footsteps shuffled out of hearing.

She shut her eyes again.

Peace—quiet—greyness. The waves were rocking her.

She did not dream. There are, by that same pity
of God, no dreams permitted in the place of refuge.
But, as she lay in peace, she watched her own memorial
thoughts rising about her, one by one, like bubbles in
a glass, like cocks crowing in the dark of the
dawn.

A white road . . . the hill-top wind panting down it
like a runner . . . dust . . . bright blue sky . . . sky-
blue succory in the gutter . . . succory is so difficult
to pick . . . tough . . . it leaves a green cut on one's
finger . . . succory in a pink vase on the mantel-piece
. . the fire's too hot for flowers . . . hot buttered
toast . . . the armchair wants mending . . . the horse-
hair tickles one's ears as one lies back in it and warms
one's toes and watches the rain drowning the fields
outside . . . empty winter fields, all tousled and tus-
socky from cow dung . . . grey skies . . . snow . . .
not a soul in sight . . . and succory in a pink vase on
the mantel-piece . . . because one's back in Eden . . .
summer and winter are all one in Eden . . . picking
buttercups in Eden as one used to do . . . all the fields
grown full of buttercups . . . fifty buttercups make a

bunch . . fifty golden buttercups with the King's head on them . . . hurry up with the buttercups . . . one more bunch of buttercups will buy back Eden—Eden —ah !

So, with a long gasping sigh would come the end. "Eden—" and the longing would be upon her, tearing like a wild beast at her eyes and her throat and her heart—"I want to go home. Oh God, let me go home ! Let me out ! Let me out ! I want to go home——"

The chapter ended.

"And does she?" I looked up at the Baxter girl. "I'm always afraid of a bad ending. Does she get back in the end?"

The Baxter girl fluttered through the pages.

"The money's stolen first—a man takes it— while she's asleep—— Oh, it's beastly, that scene. She has to save it all up again. It takes her years. But—oh, yes, she does go back."

"The railway journey," said Miss Howe. "Do you remember?"

"If you want happy endings—" the Baxter girl flattened out the last page with a jerk—"there you are !"

I read over her shoulder. The strong scent that hung about her seemed to float between me and the page.

"Here we are—where she gets to the station, 'Eden,' Madala calls it, but the woman calls it 'Breckonridge.'"

LEGEND

At last and at last the station-board with the familiar name flashed past her window. She thrilled. The station lamps repeated it as the train slowed down. She thought—how long the platform's grown ! . . . a bookstall ! . . . a bookstall on each side ! . . . there used not to be . . . wasn't the station smaller ? . . .

She spoke to the ticket collector shyly, blushing, like a girl going to an assignation and thinking that all the world must know it.

He answered, already catching at the ticket of the traveller behind her—

" How far to Breckonridge ? A mile, maybe—but you get the tram at the corner."

She stared. She would have questioned him again, but the throng of people pressed her forward.

A tram through the village ? . . . queer ! . . . not that it mattered to her . . . she would take the old short cut through the fields outside the station yard. . There was a stile . . . and a wild cherry tree. . . .

She left the yard, the unfamiliar yard with asphalt and motors and a great iron bridge, crossed the road, and stopped bewildered.

There were no fields.

' Station Road.' The labelled yellow villas were like a row of faces. Eyes, nose, mouth—windows, porch, steps—steps like teeth. They grinned.

In a sort of panic she ran past them down the road, a lumbering, clumsy woman. She trod on her skirt, and recovered herself with difficulty. She heard a small boy laugh and call after her. She clambered on to the tram.

" I want to go to the village—to Breckonridge——"

" It's all Breckonridge. 'Ow far ? "

She stared.

" I don't remember. He said a mile."

" Town 'All, I expect." He took his toll and passed on.

LEGEND

She turned vaguely to a neighbour.

"Town Hall? I don't remember. The road's all different. Where are the fields?"

The neighbour nodded.

"Built over. When were you here last? Thirty years? My word, you'll find changes! I notice it, even in five. Very full it's getting Good train service. My husband can get to his office under the hour."

She said dazedly—

"It was—it is—a little village."

The woman laughed.

"I daresay. But how long ago?"

"There were fields," she said under her breath. "There were flowers——"

"Here's the Town Hall. Didn't you want the Town Hall?"

Unsteadily she rose and got out. The tram clanged forward.

She stood on an island where four roads met and looked about her. The sun stared down at her, a brazen city sun. The asphalt was hot and soft under her feet. Road-menders were at work in the fair-way. They struck alternately at the chisel between them and it was as if the rain of blows fell upon her. She felt stupid and dizzy. She did not know where to turn. There was nothing left of her village, and yet the place was familiar. There were drab houses and rows of shops and a stream of traffic, and the figures of women and men—menacing, impersonal figures of men—that hurried towards her down the endless streets.

"Well?" said the Baxter girl.

"But that's not the *end?*" I said.

The Baxter girl looked at me oddly.

"Why not?" And then—"How else could it end? How would you make it end?"

"Oh, I don't mean——" I began. I hesitated. "I don't think I quite understand," I said.

That was the truth. At the time I couldn't follow it. It moved me. It swept me along. But whether it was good or bad I didn't know. I hadn't the faintest idea of what it was driving at. I felt in a vague way that the people at home wouldn't have liked it.

"What does it mean?" I said to the Baxter girl.

"That you can't eat your cake and have it, I suppose. You can get out of Eden, but you can't get back."

Anita answered her contemptuously—

"Is that all it means to you?"

And yet we had spoken very softly. But Anita bad eyes that ate up every movement in a room, and her small pretty ears never seemed to miss a significant word though ten people were talking. I had seen her glance uneasily at us and again at the two in the other room. I knew Great-aunt's mutter was too low even for her, and Kent Rehan only nodded now and then, but even that annoyed her. She lifted her own voice to be sure that they should hear all that she said, as if afraid lest, even for a moment, she should be left out of their thoughts.

"Oh!" she said loudly and contemptuously, "I tell you what *I* see."

LEGEND

She succeeded, if that pleased her. Kent Rehan raised his head and stared across at her with that impersonal expression of attention that, I was beginning to realize, could always anger her on any face. She had said a little while ago that she only cared for Miss Grey as an artist, and I believe that she believed it. But I don't think—I shall never think it true. I think Anita depended—depends, on other people more than she dreams. Poor Anita! I can see her now, her whole personality challenging those dark abstracted eyes. But she spoke to the Baxter girl—

"When Madala Grey chose *Eden Walls* for her title—when she flung it in the public face——"

I saw him give a shrug of fatigue or distaste—I couldn't tell which. Great-aunt, who had been sitting, her head on one side, with her sharp poll-parrot expression, crooked her finger at me. I went across to her and behind me I heard the Baxter girl—

"You talk as if she were in a passion——"

And Anita——

"So she was. I'm telling you. It's the wrongs, not of one woman, but of all women, of all ages of women, that burn behind it."

"Votes for Women!" It was Mr. Flood's voice.

There was a laugh and I lost an answer. I caught only a vehement blur of words, because Great-aunt had me by the wrist.

"Chatter, chatter! I can't hear 'em. What's my daughter talking about?"

111

I hesitated.

"About books, Auntie."

"Whose books?" she pounced.

"Some writer, Auntie."

"What's she saying about her, eh?" She held me bent down to her. I glanced at Kent Rehan. He was listening to us. I felt harried.

"About—oh—whether a genius—whether she was a genius——"

"Madala, eh?"

"Yes, Auntie."

I thought I heard him sigh. And at that—why, I don't know—I turned on him. I was rude, I believe. I sounded silly and cruel, I know. Yet, heaven knows, that that was the last thing I wanted to be.

I said angrily to him—

"Oh, why do you stand there and listen? Don't you see that I can't help myself? Why don't you go away? What good can it do you to stay here, to stay and listen to it all?"

Then I stopped because he looked at me for a moment, and flushed, and then did turn away, back again to his old dreary post at the street window.

Great-aunt chuckled.

"That's right, little Jenny. Take your own way with them, Jenny!"

I said—

"Let me go, Auntie dear," and I loosed her hand from my wrist and went after him; for of course

112

the instant the words were out of my mouth I was ashamed of myself. I couldn't think what had possessed me. I was badly ashamed of myself.

I came to him and said—

" Mr. Rehan—I don't mean to be rude. Great-aunt—she doesn't understand. She made me talk. It wasn't rudeness; but you stood there, and I knew—I thought I knew, what you must think, must be thinking—" (but 'feeling' was the word I meant) " and I was sorry. I was angry because I was sorry. I didn't mean to be rude."

He said—

" It's all right. I didn't think you rude."

Then I said—

" But I meant it. Why do you stay? What good can it do you? Why don't you go away from it all? "

And he—

" Where is there to go? I've been tramping all day."

" Where? "

" I don't know. Up and down streets. It's—it's blinding, it's stifling——"

" The fog is," I said quickly. But we didn't mean the fog.

He let himself down into the low wicker chair. I stood leaning against the sill, watching him.

" You're just dead tired," I said.

He nodded. Then, as if something in my words had stung him—

LEGEND

"Where else? I've always come here. Every month. It was natural to come."

" But now—" I said (and I was so urgent with him because of all their talk that drummed still in my mind like a wasps' nest)—" I'd go away if I were you. What good does it do you? They talk. It's—it's rather hateful. I've been listening. I'd go."

" Where? " he said again. And I—

" Haven't you anyone—at home? "

But as I asked I knew that he hadn't. He had the look. Oh, he wore good clothes and I knew he wasn't poor. But it was written all over him that he looked after himself and did it expensively and badly. He had, too, that other look that goes with it—of a man who has never found anyone more interesting to him than himself. And the queer part was that it didn't seem selfish in him—and I'm sure it wasn't. It was just like the way a child takes you for granted, and tells you about its own big affairs, and never guesses that you have your own little affairs too. I suppose it was a fault in him; but it made me like him. And he talked to me simply and almost as if he needed helping out; as if he'd been just anybody. I never had to help out anyone before : it had always been the other way round. I'd thought, too, that celebrated people were always superior and brilliant and overwhelming, like Anita and Mr. Flood. But he wasn't. He was as simple as A.B.C. I liked him. I did like him.

LEGEND

I felt happier, more at peace, standing there with him than I had felt since I had been in Anita's house. I think he would have gone on talking to me too, if it hadn't been for the Baxter girl. She spoilt it. She tilted back her chair yawning, and so caught sight of us, and laughed, and leaning over to Miss Howe, whispered in her ear. She was a crazy girl. At once I got up and came across to them, panic-stricken, hating her. I had to. I didn't want him worried, and you never knew what hateful thing the Baxter girl wouldn't say, and think that she was pleasing you.

But without knowing it, Anita helped me. Her voice, rising excitedly in answer to some word of Mr. Flood's, recalled the Baxter girl.

"Mystery? Of course there's a mystery! She was at the height of her promise in *Ploughed Fields*. It's as good as *Eden Walls* in matter and, technically, better still. The third book ought to have settled her place in modern literature for good and all. It ought to have been her master-piece. But what does she do? We expect a chaplet of pearls, and she gives us a daisy-chain. Isn't that a mystery worth solving? Won't people read the *Life* for that if for nothing else? Am I the only person who has asked what happened to her between her second and her third books?"

"I tell you, but you won't listen," Mr. Flood insisted. "Your romantic has become a realist and is flying from it to the resting-place of romance."

115

LEGEND

" I do listen. Just so. You use your words and
I use mine, but we mean the same thing. She's
been bruising herself against facts. She has been
walled up by facts. Her vision is gone. Now what
was, in her case, the all-obscuring fact ? "

" She was a woman," said the blonde lady. " It
could only be one thing. Don't I know the signs ?
She even lost her sense of humour."

" Yes, she did, didn't she ? " cried the Baxter
girl in a voice of relief. " Oh, I remember one day,
just before the engagement was announced——"

" As if that had anything to do with it," said
Anita scornfully.

" —and she'd been so absent-minded I couldn't
get anything out of her. I thought I knew her well
enough to tease her. I had told her all *my* affairs.
So—' I believe you're in love,' I said. ' Oh, well,
you'll get over it. It's a phase." Was there any
harm in that ? It was only repeating what you had
said to me about her, you know," she reminded
the blonde lady. " But she froze instantly. She
made no comment. She just changed the subject.
But I felt as if I had been introduced to a new
Madala. I wished I hadn't said it."

" You are a little fool, Beryl," said the blonde
lady tolerantly.

" But she *was* altered," insisted the Baxter girl.
" The old Madala would have laughed."

" Yes, she was altered," said Anita. " Her whole
attitude to herself and her work changed that
116

spring. How she horrified me one day. It was
soon after *Ploughed Fields* came out, and we were
talking about her new book, at least I was, pumping
a little I confess, and suddenly she said—'Anita,
I don't think I'll write any more. This stuff—'
she had her hands on *Eden Walls*, 'it's harsh, it's
ugly; and so's *Ploughed Fields*. Isn't it?' 'It's
true to life,' I said, 'that's the triumph of it.' 'Is
it?' she said. She looked at me in an uneasy sort
of way. And then—' I'd like to write a kind book,
a beautiful book.' I told her that she couldn't,
that she was a realist. 'That's why,' she said, 'I
don't think I'll write any more.' I laughed, of
course. Anybody would have laughed. 'Oh,' she
said, 'I mean it. I haven't an idea in my head.
I'm tired and empty. I think I shall go away for
a wander. There's always the country, anyhow.'
'Well, Madala,' I said, 'I think you're ungrateful.
You're a made woman. You've got your name :
you've got your line : you've got your own gift——'
'Oh, that!' she said, as if she were flicking off a
fly. I was irritated. It was so arrogant. 'What
more do you want?' I asked her. 'What more *can*
you want?' She said—'I don't know,' looking at
me, you know, as if she expected me to tell her. I
disliked that mood of hers. One did expect, with
a woman of her capacity, to be entertained as it
were, to have ideas presented, not to be asked to
provide them. Then she began, à propos of nothing
at all—'If I ever marry——' That startled me.

LEGEND

We'd never touched on the subject before. ' Oh,
my dear Madala,' I said, ' you must never think of
anything so—so unnecessary. For you, of all
people, it would be fatal. It would waste your time,
it would distract your thoughts, it would narrow
your outlook, it would end by spoiling your work
altogether. I've seen it happen so often. It's
terrible to me even to think of a woman with a
future like yours, throwing it away just for the——'
She interrupted me. ' I wouldn't marry for the
sake of getting married, if you mean that. Not even
for children.' "

" You didn't mean that, did you, Anita? " said
Miss Howe smiling a little.

" Certainly not. But I had always been afraid
that she might be tempted to marry for the
adventure's sake, for the mere experience, for
the——"

" Copy," said Mr. Flood. " I always said so.
Yes ? "

" ' Oh well, Madala,' I said to her, ' you know
what I think. I'm not one to quote Kipling, but—
He travels fastest who travels alone.' She looked at
me so strangely. ' Alone ? ' she said. ' Alone. It's
the cruellest word in the language. There's drowning in it.' ' Well, without conceit, Madala,' I said,
' I can affirm that I have been alone, spiritually, all
my life.' ' Ah, yes,' she said, ' but you're different.'
And that," Anita broke off, " was what I liked in
Madala. She did recognize differences. She could

118

appreciate. She wasn't absorbed in herself. She said to me quite humbly—' I'm not strong, I suppose; but I don't suffice myself. I can't bear myself sometimes. I can't bear the burden of myself. Can't you understand?' 'Frankly,' I said, 'I can't. I'm a modern woman, and the modern woman is a pioneer. She's the Columbus of her own individuality. She must be. It's her career. It's her destiny.' She answered me pettishly, like a naughty child—' I don't want to be a pioneer.' ' You're that,' I said, ' already, whether you want to be or not.' Then she said to me, with that dancing, impish look that her eyes and her lips and her white teeth ı s ·d to manage between them—' All right! If I've got to be, I will. But I'll be a pioneer in my own way. I swear I'll shock the lot of you."

" *Oho !* " said Mr. Flood with exaggerated unction.

"Exactly ! " Anita gave his agreement such eager welcome. " That put me on the qui-vive. Knowing her as I did, it was a very strong hint. I awaited developments. Frankly, I was prepared for a scandal, a romance, anything you please in the way of extravagance. That's why the Carey marriage, that tameness, upset me so. It was not what I was expecting. Really, I don't know which was more of a shock to me, *The Resting-place* or the marriage. Hardly had I recovered from the one when——"

" Oh, *The Resting-place* was the shock of my life

119

too." He giggled. " I mourned, I assure you that
I mourned over it. That opening, you know—
' There was once '—And the end again—' So they
were married and had children and lived happily
ever after.' Pastiche ! And then to be invited to
wade through a conscientious account of how they
achieved it ! Too bad of Madala ! As if the poor
but virtuous artist's-model weren't a drug on
the market already ! And the impecunious artist
himself—*stooping*, you know ! Oh, I sat in ashes."

Miss Howe clapped her hands.

" Jasper, I love you. I *do* love you. Did she
pull your leg too ? Both legs ? She did ! She did !
Oh, there's only one Madala ! "

Mr. Flood's vanity was in his cheeks while she
rattled on.

" Darling Jasper, I thought better of you ! Can't
you see th whole thing's a skit ? Giving the jam-
pot public what they wanted ! Why, it's been out
a vear and they're sucking the spoon still. It's
the resting-place ! Ask the libraries ! Oh, can't
you see ? "

" If it is parody," said Mr. Flood slowly, " then,
I admit, it's unique."

" What else ? You'll not deny humour to
her ? "

" I do ! " the blonde lady nodded her head.
" Once a woman is in love she's quite hopeless."

" I don't see how parody could be in question,"
Anita broke in. " Anybody reading the book care-

fully must see that she's in earnest. That's the tragedy of it."

" The literary tragedy ? "

" Not only literary. The psychological value is enormous. It's not art, it's record. It's photography. That happened. That happened, tragically, to Madala. Oh, not the trimmings, of course, not the happy-ever-after. But to me it's perfectly clear that that lapse into *Family Herald* romance has had its equivalent in Madala's own life. I've always felt a certain weakness in her character, you know—a certain sentimentalism."

" In the author of *Eden Walls?* " said Miss Howe contemptuously.

" No, dear lady ! But in the author of *The Resting-place.*" Mr. Flood had recovered himself.

" Skit, I tell you, skit ! " she insisted. And they continued to bicker in undertones while Anita summed up the situation.

" No, my theory is this—Madala Grey met some man——"

" Carey ? " asked Mr. Flood, dividing his allegiance.

" No, Carey comes later. There was — an episode——"

" Episodes ? " he amended.

" Possibly. But an episode anyhow, that I place myself at the end of the *Ploughed Fields* period. It may have been later, it may have been the following summer while she was working at *The Resting-*

place. I'm open to conviction there. But an episode there must have been. In *The Resting-place* she wrote it down as it ought to have happened."

" Why ought ? "

" Well, obviously it didn't happen or she wouldn't have become Mrs. Carey."

" The gentleman loved and rode away, you mean ? "

" Something of the sort. Something went wrong."

" I see." Miss Howe was interested. " It's a theory, anyhow. And then in sheer savage irony at her own weakness——"

" Not a bit. In sheer weak longing——"

" I see. If your theory is correct—I don't know what you base it on——"

" Internal evidence," said Anita airily.

" Then I can imagine that *The Resting-place* was a relief to write. Poor Madala ! "

" And then," concluded Anita triumphantly, " then appears Carey, and she's too worn out, too exhausted with her own frustrated emotions to care what happens. The book's in her head still, and she her own heroine. He appears to her—I admit that it's possible that even Carey might appear to her— as a refuge, a resting-place."

" Yes, but you don't like Mr. Carey," said the Baxter girl. " But if Madala did ? Isn't it possible that in Madala's eyes——? Why shouldn't the hero be Mr. Carey himself ? "

LEGEND

Anita's eyes were bright with the cold anger that she always showed at the name.

"My good girl, you know nothing about John Carey, or you'd rule that out. Have you ever seen him? I thought not. And yet you *have* seen him. All day. Every day. When you talk of the man in the street, whom do you mean? What utterly common-place face is in your mind? Shall I tell you what is in mine? John Carey. Ordinary! Ordinary! The apotheosis of the uninspired! Oh, I haven't any words. Look for yourself." She rummaged furiously in the half-opened desk and flung out a fading snapshot on a mount. "There he is! That's the thing she married!"

"What's he doing in your holy of holies?" Mr. Flood's eyes seemed to bore into her desk.

Anita, still thrusting down the overflowing papers, answered coldly—

"Madala sent it to Mother. She said that it wasn't good enough but that it would give her an idea."

"It certainly gives one an idea," said the blonde lady languorously.

"And then she put in a post-script that it didn't do him justice because the sun was in his eyes. Defiantly, as it were. Isn't that significant? She'd never own to a mistake. Pride! She had the devil's own pride. Look at the way she took her reviews! And in this case she would be bound to defend him. She'd defend anything she'd once taken under her wing."

LEGEND

"Well, you know,"·drawled the blonde lady, her eyes on the photograph, "according to this he topped her by two inches. I don't somehow see him *under* Madala's wing." And then—"After all, there's something rather fascinating in bone and muscle."

"Yes, and I don't see," the Baxter girl hurried into defiance, "honestly I don't see, Miss Serle, why she shouldn't have been in love with him. Of course, it's not a clever face, but it's good-tempered, and it's good-looking, and there's a twinkle. Madala loved a twinkle. And I don't see——"

Anita crushed her.

"We're discussing the standards of Madala Grey."

"That's not the point either, Anita." Mr. Flood would sometimes rouse himself to defend the Baxter girl. "You know something. You own to it. What do you know?"

"Simply that she was in love with someone else. I've papers that prove it. Now it was either some man whom none of us know, whom for some reason she wouldn't let us know, or——" she hesitated. Then she began again—"Mind you, I don't commit myself, but—has the likeness never struck you? *Hugh Barrington* in *The Resting-place* and——?" Her eyes flickered towards Kent Rehan.

Mr. Flood whistled.

"Be careful, Anita."

"He?" Miss Howe laughed, but kindly. "He's lost to the world. He'll be worse than ever now."'

124

LEGEND

" There ! " Anita dropped upon the sentence like a hawk upon a heather bird. " You see ! You say that ! And yet you tell me there was nothing—nothing—between them ? Didn't she rave about him ? his talents ? his personality ? his charm ? And then she goes and writes the story of an artist's-model ! "

Miss Howe laughed again.

" When a thing's as obvious as that, it probably isn't so. Besides, the artist's-model marries the artist."

" Exactly. She leaves them, and us, cloyed with love in a cottage. I repeat, the artist's-model marries the artist because Madala Grey didn't. It's the merest shadow of a solution as yet, but—isn't that a living portrait in *The Resting-place?* Oh, I know it by heart——

" Maybe it was his height that gave you the impression, less of weakness than of vagueness, as if his high forehead touched cloud-land, and were obscured by dreams; for his cold eyes guarded his mind from you, and his dark beard hid his mouth."

" You *do* know it by heart ! " said Miss Howe.

" Of course I know it by heart. It was the first clue. Can anybody read those lines without recognizing him ? "

The Baxter girl persisted—

" But I don't see it. Oh, of course it is like him—but because she borrowed his face, the story needn't

125

be about him. Why couldn't she just imagine the story? If she was a genius?"

"That remains the point," said Mr. Flood.

"She was," insisted Anita stubbornly.

Miss Howe smiled and said nothing.

He continued—

"The mere fact that she was a genius would prevent such a descent into milk and sugar, unless she were money-making or love-sick."

The blonde lady spoke—

"Just so! Love-sick—sick of love—savage with love—savaging her holy of holies. A parody. Lila's right."

But Miss Howe shook her head.

"No, no. I didn't mean that sort of parody. Madala may have had her emotions, but she'd always be good-tempered about them. She's laughing at herself in *The Resting-place* as well as at us."

"But why do you cavil at it so?" said the Baxter girl slowly.

"Only at its plain meaning. Grant the parody and——"

"But why can't you just read it as it stands? Why do you say sentimental? I—I liked it."

Anita took the book from her hand.

"But, my dear child, *any*body can write this sort of thing. Where's the passage the ladies' papers rave about, where they have a day on the river together?" She whipped over the pages while I said to the Baxter girl—

LEGEND

"What is it? What's it about? What's the plot?"

"Oh, there isn't any. That's what they complain of. It's just a little artist's-model who sits to an elderly, broken-down dreamer, and thinks him a god. The duke and door-mat touch. It's just how two people fall in love and find it out. It's as simple as A.B.C. But people ate it when it came out."

"Treacle, I tell you," insisted Mr. Flood.

Anita overheard him.

"Exactly! Listen to this—

. . . and they landed at last in a meadow of brilliant, brook-fed grass.

She had no words in which to say a thousand times 'How beautiful!' Words? She had never known a country June. She had never seen whole hedges clotted with bloom, she had never in all her life breathed the perfume of the may or heard a lark's ecstasy. She had never—and to her simplicity there was no break in the chain of thought—she had never before been alone with him, unpaid, not his servant but his equal and companion. How should she have words?

She sat in the grass with the tall ox-eyes nodding at her elbow and looked at him from under her hat with a little eased sigh. This, after the dust of the journey, of the day, of her life, was bliss. She prepared herself for this bliss, deliberately, as she did everything. She was too poor and too hungry to be wasteful of her happiness : she must have every crumb. Therefore she had looked first at herself, critically, with her trained eye, fingering the frill of her blouse, flinging a scatter

127

of skirt across her dusty city feet, lest her poverty
should jar his thoughts of her

Then she looked at him. She saw him for a moment
with undazzled eyes, the blue sky enriched with clouds
behind him. She was saying to herself—' I'm not a
fool. I can see straight. I know what he is. He's
just an ordinary man in a hot, black suit. He stoops,
I suppose. He's worn out with work. He'll never be
young again. And there's nothing particular about
him. Then what makes me like him? But I do. I
do. He has only to turn and smile at me——'

Then he turned and smiled at her, and it seemed to
her that the glamour of the gilded day passed over
and into him as he smiled, glorifying him so that she
caught her breath at his beauty. She knew her happiness. She knew herself and him. He was the sum of
the blue sky and green, green grass, and the shining
waters and the flowers with their sweet smell, and the
singing birds and the hum of the little things of the air.
All beauty was summed up in him: he was food to
her and sunshine and music: he was her absolute good:
and she thought that someone ought to see that his
socks were mended properly, for there was a great
ladder down one ankle, darned with wrong-coloured
wool.

" Well ? " She shut the book.

" I like it," said the Baxter girl stubbornly.

Mr. Flood twisted uneasily in his seat.

" Oh, pretty, of course. Of course it's pleasant
enough in a way. But Madala oughtn't to be
pretty. Think of the stuff she *can* do."

" But can't you see," Miss Howe broke in. " how
it parodies the slush and sugar school ? "

Anita shook her head.

" She used another manner when she was ironical. I wish you were right. Oh, you may be—I must consider—but I'm afraid that she is in earnest. That phrase now—' The green, green grass,' (why double the adjective?) ' the shining waters, the singing birds'—pitiful! And that anti-climax—' He was her absolute good : and she thought that someone ought to see that his socks were mended properly.' I ask you—is it art? "

" Not as serious work, of course," said Miss Howe, " but——"

" I wish I could think so," said Anita.

" Well, I wish I could do it," said the Baxter girl. " What do you say, Jenny? "

But it had brought back the country to me. It had brought back home. I hadn't anything to say to them.

" And she wouldn't discuss it, you know. She came in after supper that night, just as I was reading the last chapter. It had only been out a day. There she sat, where you are now, Lila, smiling, with her hands in her lap and her eyes fixed on her hands, waiting for me to finish."

" Oh—" Miss Howe gave a little gushing scream, " that reminds me—d'you know, Anita, somebody actually told me that nobody had seen *The Resting-place* before it was published, not even you. I was amused. I denied it, of course."

" Why? " said Anita coldly.

129

LEGEND

Miss Howe screamed again.

"Then you didn't? Oh, my dear?"

"Emancipation with a vengeance," said Mr. Flood.

"It had to come, Anita," said Miss Howe with deadly sympathy.

"It was not that. It was only—she was so extraordinarily sensitive about *The Resting-place*—unlike herself altogether. I think, I've always thought that she herself knew how unworthy it was of her. She—what's the use of disguising it?—she, at least, had a value for my judgment," her eyes, wandering past Miss Howe, brooded upon the Baxter girl, "and she knew what my judgment would be. She owned it. She anticipated it. I had shut the book, you know, quietly. She sat so still that I thought she was asleep. She had had one of those insane mornings——"

"Of course. She used to take a crowd of children into the country, didn't she?"

"Once a week. Slum children."

"I know. 'To eat buttercups,' she told me," said Miss Howe.

"It was ridiculous, you know. She couldn't afford it. Look at the way she lived! I always said to her, 'If you can afford mad extravagances of that sort, you can afford a decent flat in a decent neighbourhood'——"

"Oh, but I loved those rooms," said the Baxter girl, "with the Spanish leather screen round the wash-hand-stand."

Anita glanced behind her.

"Ah, you've noticed? I happened to admire it one day and—you know what she is—'Would you like it? Why, of course, it would just suit the rest of your things. Oh, you must have it. I'd like you to. It's far too big for this room.' 'Oh,' I said, 'if you want it housed——' So that's how it comes to be here. One couldn't hurt her feelings. And you know, it was quite unsuitable to lodging-house furniture."

Miss Howe laughed.

"It disguised the wash-hand-stand. That was all Madala cared. Only then she always took you round to show you how beautifully it did disguise it."

"Typical," said Mr. Flood. "Her reserves were topsy-turvy."

"But she had her reserves," said Miss Howe quickly.

"I doubt that," he answered her.

"Oh, but she had." Anita recovered her place in the talk. "Curious reserves. You know how she came to me over *Eden Walls* and *Ploughed Fields.* I saw every chapter. But as I was telling you, she wouldn't hear a criticism of *The Resting-place.* That evening she pounced on me. She was as quick as light. She said—'You don't like it! I knew you wouldn't! Never mind, Anita. Forget it! Put it in the fire! You like me. What do the books matter?' She'd been watching me all the time."

131

"She had eyes in the back of her head," said Miss Howe.

"Kind eyes," said the Baxter girl.

"And I assure you she wouldn't have said another word on the subject if I hadn't insisted. I told her not to be ridiculous. How could I help being disappointed? How could I separate her from her work? I was disappointed, bitterly. I made it clear. I said to her—'Well, Madala, all I can say is that if your future output is to be on a level with this—this pot-boiler——"

"It's not a pot-boiler," said the Baxter girl loudly and quite rudely. "I don't know exactly what it is, but it's not a pot-boiler."

Anita stared her down.

"'—pot-boiler,' I said, 'then—I wash my hands of you.' I wanted to rouse her. I couldn't understand her."

"Well?" said Miss Howe.

They all laughed.

"Oh, you can guess." Anita was petulant, but she, too, laughed a little. "You know her way. She just sat smiling and twisting a ring that she wore and looking like a scolded child."

"But what did she say?" said the Baxter girl.

"Nothing to the point. 'Oh,' she said, 'but Anita, if I'd never written anything, wouldn't you be just as fond of me?' Such a silly thing to say! She was distressing at times. She embarrassed me. Fond of her! She knew my interests were intellectual. Fond of her! For a woman of her brains her standard of values was childish."

" But you were fond of her, you know," said Miss Howe.

" Oh, as for that—there was something about her—she had a certain way—— After all, if it gave her pleasure to be demonstrative, it was easier to acquiesce. But she made a fetish of such things. I was only trying to explain to her, as I tell you, that it was quite impossible to separate creator and creatures, and that to me she was *Eden Walls* and *Ploughed Fields*, and if you believe me, she was upon me like a whirlwind, shaking me by the shoulders, and crying out—' No, no, stop! You're to stop! It's me you like, not the books. I hate them. I hate all that. I shall get away from all that one day.' And I said—' I don't wonder you're ashamed of *The Resting-place*. I advise you to get to work at once on your new book. You'll find that if you pull yourself together——' And all she said was —' Nita! Nita! *Don't!*' And she looked at me in such a curious way——"

" How ? " somebody said.

" I don't know—laughing—despairing. She'd no right to look at me like that. It was I who was in despair."

" I'd like to have seen you two," said Miss Howe.

" I didn't know what had got into her. Of course I blame myself. I ought to have followed it out.

I might have prevented things. But I was annoyed and she saw it, and she——"

Miss Howe twinkled.

" She wouldn't let you be annoyed with her long What did she do with you, Anita ? "

" She ? I don't know what you mean. We changed the subject. And as a matter of fact I was much occupied at the time with the *Anthology*." She paused. " She had excellent taste," said Anita regretfully. " Naturally I reserved to myself the final decision, but——"

" Just so," said Mr. Flood.

" Be quiet, Jasper." The blonde lady's draperies dusted his shoulder intimately.

" She'd brought me a delicious thing of Lady Nairn's, I remember, that I'd overlooked. And from talking of the *Anthology* we came, somehow, to talking about me. Yes—" Anita gave an embarrassed half laugh—" She began to talk to me, turning the tables as it were—about myself. She'd never, in all the years I'd known her, taken such a tone. Astonishing ! As if—as if I were the younger." She stared at them, as one combating an unuttered criticism. " I—liked it," said Anita defiantly. " There was nothing impertinent. It was heartening. She made me feel that one person in the world, at least, knew me—knew my work. I realized, suddenly, that while I had been studying her, she must have been studying me, that she understood my capacities, my limitations, my

possibilities, almost as well as I did myself. The
relief of it—indescribable! She was extraordinarily
plain-spoken. As a rule, you know, I thought her
manner——"

"Insincere?" said the Baxter girl. "Yes, I've
heard people say that."

"It had that effect. It didn't seem possible that
she could like everyone as much as she made them
think she did. But with me, at least, she was always
frankness itself. She believes, you know,—she
believed, that is, that all my work so far, even the
Anthology and the *Famous Women* series, not to
mention the lighter work, is still preliminary: that
my—" she hesitated—"my master-piece, she called
it, was still to come. She said that, though she
appreciated all my work, I hadn't 'found myself.' Yes! from that child to me it was amusing.
But right, you know. She said that my line, whether
I dealt with a period or a person, would always be
critical, but that I'd never had a big success because
so far I'd been merely critical: that I'd never
become identified with my subject: that I'd always
remained aloof—inhuman. Yes, she said that. A
curious theory—but it interested me. But she said
that it was only the real theme I needed, the en-
grossing subject. She said that my chance would
come: that 'she felt it in her bones.' I can hear
her voice now—'Don't you worry, Nita! It'll
come to you one day. A big thing. Biography, I
shouldn't wonder. And I shall sit and say—I told

you so—I told you so ! ' Yes, she talked like that.
Oh, it's nothing when I repeat it, but if you knew
how it seemed to pour new life into me. It was
the belief in her voice ! "

" She always believed in you," said Miss Howe
with a certain harshness. " Insincere ! You should
have heard her talk of your *Famous Women !* " And
then—" Yes. She believed in you right enough."

" More than I did in her that night. I couldn't
forget *The Resting-place*. It lay on the table, and
every now and then, when I felt most comfort in
her, my eyes would fall on it, and it would jar me.
She felt it too. When I saw her off at last—it had
grown very late—she stopped at the gate and
turned and came running back. I thought that
she had forgotten her handbag. She nearly always
forgot her handbag. But no, it was *The Resting-
place* that was on her mind. It was—' Nita ! try
it again. Maybe you'd like it better.' And then—
' Nita ! I enjoyed writing it so.' ' That's something,
at any rate,' I said, not wanting, you know, to be
unkind. Then she said—' I wish you liked it.
Because, you know, Nita—' and stopped as if she
wanted to tell me something and couldn't make
up her mind. ' Well, what ? ' I said. It was cold
on the steps. She hesitated. She looked at me.
For an instant I had an absurd impression that she
was going to cry. Then she kissed me. She'd
kissed me good-night once already, though, you
know, we never did as a rule. And then, off she

went without another word. I was quite bewildered
by her. I nearly called her back; but it was one
of those deep dark blue nights : it seemed to swallow
her up at once. But I heard her footsteps for a
long while after—dragging steps, as if she were
tired. I wasn't. It was as if she had put something into me. I went back into the house and I
worked till daylight. And all the next day I
worked—worked well. I felt, I remember, so hope-
ful, so full of power. By the evening I had quite a
mass of material to show her, if she came. I half
expected her to come. But instead—" she fumbled
among her papers—" I got this."

It was a sheet of note-paper, a sheet that looked
as if it had been crushed into a ball and then
smoothed out again for careful folding. Anita's
fingers were still ironing out the crinkled edge while
she read it aloud.

" I want to tell you something. I tried to tell you
yesterday, but somehow I couldn't. It oughtn't to be
difficult, yet all this afternoon I've been writing to you
in an exercise book, and crossing out, and re-phrasing,
and putting in again as carefully and dissatisfiedly as
if it were Opus 4. I wish it were, because then you'd
be very much pleased with Madala Grey and forget
the dreadful shock of Opus 3 ! I was always afraid
you wouldn't like it, and sorry, because I like it more
than all my other work put together. Have you never
even begun to guess why ? But how should you, when
I didn't know myself until after it was finished ? Coming
events, I suppose. It's quite true—one isn't overtaken

137

LEGEND

by fate : one prepares one's own fate : one carries it about inside one, like a child. I hear you say—' Can't you come to the point ? ' No, I can't. Partly because I'm afraid of what you'll say, because I'm afraid you'll be disappointed, and partly, selfishly, because there is a queer pleasure in beating about the bush that bears my flower. It's too beautiful to pick straight away in one rough snatch of a sentence. Am I selfish? You've been so kind to me. I know you will be sorry and that troubles me. And yet—Anita, I am going to be married. You met him once in the churchyard at home, do you remember ? I've seen him now and then when I took the children down there in the summer. He——

There's something scratched out here," said Anita.

" I think we shall be happy. When you get accustomed to the idea I hope you will like him."

She paused.

" Now what do you make of that ? " said Anita.

" It explains the expeditions with the children," said Mr. Flood. " They were always too—philanthropic, to be quite—eh ? "

" Oh, but she began those outings ages ago," said Miss Howe quickly.

" Besides," said Anita, " she didn't go every week that summer. That's the point. She told me herself that she was so busy that she had to get help—one of those mission women. Now why was she so busy ? "

" Diversions in the country *and* attractions in town ? " said Mr. Flood. " It all takes time."

188

Anita nodded.

" You think that? So do I. *And* attractions in town! Exactly! At any rate I shall make that the big chapter, the convincing chapter, of the *Life*. I think I shall be able to prove that that summer was the climax of her affairs. I grant you that she met Carey that summer, but as she says herself, a few times only. We must look nearer home than Carey."

" Oh, but there's such a thing as love at first .sight," protested the Baxter girl, and Anita dealt with her in swift parenthesis—

" I was there when they first met. Shouldn't I have realized——?" And then, continuing—"Well, reckon up my points. To begin with—the difference in her that we all noticed, the restlessness, the—unhappiness one might almost say, the aloofness—oh, don't you know what I mean? as if she didn't belong to us any more."

" As if she didn't belong to herself any more."

" Yes, yes, that's even more what I mean. Then comes the fact that we saw so little of her. What did she do with her time? Writing *The Resting-place*, was her explanation, but—is that gospel? Do you really believe that she sat at home writing and dreaming all those long summer days and nights, except when she was—eating buttercups—with Carey and her chaperons? And then comes *The Resting-place* with its appalling falling-off, and following on that, this letter, this sudden engage-

ment. Now doesn't it look—I ask you, doesn't
it look as if something had been going on behind
all our backs and had at last come to a head?"

"Oh, that she was in love is certain," said Mr.
Flood. "Was there ever a woman of genius who
wasn't?"

"Exactly. It's a moral certainty. And this
letter to me proves that, whoever it was, it wasn't
Carey. 'I think we shall be happy.' 'I hope
you will like him.' Is that the way a woman writes
of her first love or her first lover?"

"Oh, but that sentence just before——" the
Baxter girl stretched out her hand for the letter—
"'The bush that bears my flower——'" She spoke
sympathetically; but it jarred me. I wondered
now I should feel if I thought that the Baxter girl
would ever read my letters aloud.

"Ah, that's the literary touch. Madala could
never resist embroideries. Besides—she wants to
confuse me. That means nothing. But here, you
see——" she took the letter out of the Baxter girl's
hand—"as soon as she comes to the point, the real
point, the confession, the apologia—then the baldest
sentences. Try to remember that Madala Grey has
written one of the strongest love scenes of the
decade, and all she can say of the man she is to
marry is—'I hope you will like him.'"

"Hm! It's curious!" Miss Howe was frowning.

"Isn't it? And then you know, the whole
manner of the engagement was so unlike her usual
140

triumphant way. She always swept one along, didn't she? But in the matter of the marriage she seems, as far as I can make out, to have been perfectly passive. She left everything to the man —arrangements—furniture—I imagine she even bought her clothes to please him. And the wedding itself—no reception, no presents, no notice to anyone, so sudden, so private. Not a word even to her oldest friends——"

Great-aunt stirred in her corner.

"—there was something so furtive about it all: as if she were running away from something."

Miss Howe sat up.

"D'you mean?—what do you mean, Anita? Are you hinting——?"

Anita looked at her in a puzzled way that relieved me, I hardly knew why.

"Why, only that it carries out my theory—of Carey as a refuge."

"From what?"

"Life — frustration — what did you think I meant?"

"I don't know. Nothing. It was my evil mind, I suppose." She flushed.

"How she harps on the child!" the Baxter girl carried it on.

"That's a mere simile——" said Miss Howe swiftly.

"But a queer simile!"

"The marriage *was* sudden," said Mr. Flood from

LEGEND

the floor in his silky voice. " Anita's theory has its points."

" A seven months' child ! " It was the first word that the blonde lady had said for some time. There was something sluggishly cold, slimily cold, in her abstracted voice.

Anita started.

" I never suggested that," she said sharply. But there was a quiver in her voice that was more excitement than anger.

" My dear lady, nobody suggests anything. We are only remarking that the union of our Madala and her 'refuge'—the soubriquet is yours, by the way—was as surprising as it was—er—sudden. That was your idea ? " He turned to the shadows and from them the blonde lady nodded, smiling.

At the time, you know, I didn't understand them. They were so quick and allusive. They said more in jerks and nods and pauses than in actual speech. But I saw the smile on that woman's face, and heard the way he said ' our Madala.' I felt myself growing angry and panic-stricken, and I was quite helpless. I just went across the room to that big man sitting dully in his corner, in his dream, and I caught his arm and cried to him under my breath—

" You must come. You must come and stop them. They're talking about her. Come quickly. They—they're saying beastly things."

He gave me one look. Then he got up and went swiftly from one room to the other. But swiftly

142

as he moved and I followed, someone else was there before us to fight that battle.

It was Great-aunt Serle.

She was a heavy old woman and feeble. She never stirred as a rule without a helping arm; but somehow she had got herself out of her seat and across the floor to the table, and there she stood, her knitting gripped as if it were a weapon, the long thread of it stretched and taut from the ball that had rolled round the chair-leg, her free hand and her tremulous head jerking and snapping and poking at that amazed assembly as she rated them—

" I won't allow such talk. Anita, I won't have it. If I let you bring home friends—ought to know better! And you——" the blonde lady was spitted, as it were, on that unerring finger, " you're a wicked woman. That's what you are—a wicked, scandalous woman. And you, Anita, ought to be ashamed of yourself, to let her talk so of my girl. Such a woman! Paint and powder! Envy, hatred, malice! And in my house too! Tell her to wash her face!" She glowered at them.

There was a blank pause and then a sound somewhere, like the end of a spurting giggle. It must have been the Baxter girl. There was a most uncomfortable moment, before Anita cried out " Mother!" in a horrified voice, and Miss Howe said " Beryl!" in a voice not quite as horrified.

But the blonde lady sat through it all quite

143

calmly, smiling and moistening her lips. At last
she drawled out—

"Nita! Your dear mother's quite upset. So
sorry, Nita!" Then, a very little lower, but we
could all hear it—"Poor dear Nita! Quite a trial
for poor dear Nita!"

But Anita had jumped up. She was very much
flustered and annoyed. I think, too, that she was
startled. I know that I was startled. Great-aunt
didn't look like herself. She was like a witch in a
picture-book, and her voice had been quite strong
and commanding.

Anita tried to quiet her and get her away.

"Mother! You must be quiet! D'you hear
me, Mother? You don't know what you're saying. You've been up too long. You're overdone.
It's time you went to bed."

She took her firmly by the arm. But Great-aunt
struggled with her.

"I won't. Leave me alone. It's your fault,
Anita. You sat and listened. You let them talk
that way about my girl."

"Now, Mother, what nonsense! Your girl!
Madala's not your daughter." And then, in
apology—"She's always confusing us. She gets
these ideas."

"Not mine? Ah! That's all you know!
'Anita upstairs?' That's how she'd come running
in to me. 'Are you busy, Mrs. Serle?' Always
looked in to my room first. Brought me violets.

Talked. Told me all her troubles. *You* never
knew. Not mine, eh? Didn't I see her married,
my pretty girl? 'Hole-and-corner business!'
That's what you tell them? 'Nobody knew.'
But I knew."

Anita's hand dropped from her mother's arm.
She stared at her.

"You, Mother? You there?" And then,
angrily, "Oh, I don't believe it."

"Don't believe it, eh? But it's true, for all I'm
lumber in my own house. I'm to go to bed before
the company comes, before she comes. Don't she
want to see me then? Who pinned her veil for her
and kissed her and blessed her, and took her to
church, and gave her to him? Not you, my
daughter. She didn't come to you for that."
And then, with a slacking and a wail, "Eh, but we
were never to tell!"

"Mother, you'd better come to bed. I——"
there was the faintest suggestion of menace in her
voice—"I'll talk to you tomorrow."

The old woman shrank away.

"I won't come. I know. You want me out of
the way. You don't want me to see her. What
are you going to say about me? You'll say things
to her about me. I've heard you."

Quite obviously Anita restrained herself.

"Now, Mother, you know you don't mean that."

"Hush!" Great-aunt pulled away her hand.
"Quiet, child, quiet! Wasn't that the cab? I've

listened all the evening, all the long evening." Her
old voice thinned and sharpened to a chirp. "Soft,
soft, the wheels go by. The wheels never stop.
Wait till the wheels stop. It's the fog that's
keeping her. There's fog everywhere. Maybe she's
lost in the fog." Then she chuckled to herself.
"Naughty girl to be so late. But she's always
late. Why should I go to bed? I've got to finish
my knitting, Nita. Only two rows, Nita. They'll
just last me till she comes." And then, "Anita,
she will come?"

Anita turned to the others.

"Don't be alarmed. It's nothing. I'm afraid
she hasn't realized——" She began again—"Now,
Mother! It's bed-time, Mother dear."

"'Dear'—'dear'—why do you speak kindly?
Madala's not here to listen." And then—"Nita,
Nita child, let me stay till she comes."

Anita was quite patient with her, and quite
unyielding.

"Now listen, Mother! It's no use waiting.
Come upstairs with me. She won't——" her voice
altered, "she can't come tonight."

Beside me Kent Rehan spoke—

"I can't stand it," he said. "I can't stand it.
I can't stand it." He didn't seem to know that he
was speaking.

But Great-aunt heard his voice if she didn't hear
the words. She broke away from Anita and went
shuffling over the floor towards him with blind

146

movements. She would have fallen if he hadn't been beside her in an instant, holding her.

" Kent, d'you hear her? You know my daughter. You know Madala too. You speak to her! You tell her! Madala always comes, doesn't she? always comes. You tell her that! I want to see Madala. Very good to me, Madala. Brought me a bunch of violets."

Anita followed.

" Kent, for goodness' sake, try to help me. She'll make herself ill. I shall have her in bed for days. Now, Mother——Now come, Mother!"

Great-aunt clung to his arm.

" She's not kind. My daughter's very hard on me."

For the first time Anita showed signs of agitation. She was almost appealing.

" Kent! You mustn't believe her. It's not fair. You see my position. One has to be firm. And you don't know how trying—— What am I to do? Shall I tell her? She's as obstinate—I'll never get her to bed. Ought I to tell her? She'll have to be told sooner or later. She'll have to realize——"

He said—

" I'll talk to her if you like."

Anita looked at him intently.

" It's good of you. She has always listened to you. Since you and I were children together. Do you remember, Kent? Yes, you talk to her."

147

LEGEND

"What's she saying?" demanded Great-aunt. Her old eyes were bright with suspicion. "Talking you over, eh? Talk anyone over, my daughter will—my clever daughter. So clever. Madala thinks so too. 'Dripping with brains.' That's what Madala said. Made me laugh. Quite true, though. Hasn't Madala come yet?"

"Now, look here, Mrs. Serle——" he put his arm round her bent shoulders, "it's very foggy, you know, and it's very late. Nobody could travel— nobody could come tonight. You'll believe us, won't you?"

"Wait! What's that?" She stood a moment, her finger raised, listening intently. Then she straightened her bowed body and looked up at him. One so seldom saw her face lifted, shone upon by any light, that that alone, I suppose, was enough to change her. For changed she was—her countenance so wise and beaming that I hardly knew her. "Now I know," she said, "she will come. Wait for her, Kent. She will come. I—I hear her coming. She's not so far from us. She's not so far away."

They stared at each other for a moment, the man and the old woman. Then her face dropped forward again, downward into its accustomed shadow, as he said to her—

"It's too late, Mrs. Serle. She won't come—now. Not now any more. And Anita thinks—truly you're very tired, aren't you? Now aren't you?"

"Very tired," she quavered.

148

"I know you are. Won't you let me help you upstairs?"

"And stay a bit?" she said, clutching at him. "Stay and talk to me?"

"Yes, yes," he humoured her.

"About Madala?"

He was very white.

"About Madala. Anita, take her other arm. That's the way."

They helped her out of the room, and we heard their slow progress up the stairs.

It was the blonde lady who broke the silence with her tinkling laugh—

"Poor dear Nita!"

"Kent's a good sort," said Miss Howe.

"What's Hecuba to him now?" Mr. Flood's smile glinted from one to another.

"A very old friend," said the blonde lady. "You heard what dear Nita said to him."

"'Children together!' I didn't know that." He was still smiling.

"And they always kept in touch," put in Miss Howe.

"Trust Nita for that," said the blonde lady.

Miss Howe nodded.

"She told me once that from the first she realized that he would do big things."

"So Nita kept in touch!" Mr. Flood laughed outright.

"But it's only the last fe~ years that she's

been able to produce him at will, like a conjuror's rabbit."

"Since Madala's advent, you mean," said the blonde lady.

"'Will you walk into my parlour,' said Anita to the fly. 'It's a literary parlour——'" murmured Mr. Flood. And then—"No. Kent's not likely to have walked in without a honey-pot in the parlour. Madala must have been useful."

"That's what Miss Serle will never forgive her, *I* think," said the Baxter girl.

"What?"

"That she was useful. Do *you* believe in the other man?"

"The unknown influence?" His eyes narrowed. "Hm!"

"And yet of course there's been someone." The Baxter girl never quite deserted Anita, even in her absence.

The blonde lady nodded.

"Of course. Nita's always nearly right. The influence—the adventures—the *mariage de convenance*—she's got it all so pat—and the man too. She knows well enough; yet she fights against it. She won't have it. I wonder why. 'Very old friends' I suppose." She laughed again. "But of course it was Kent. Can't you see that's why Nita hates her? What a *Life* it will be! I just long for it to come out. Nita's a comedy."

"A tragedy."

" Nita ?　My dear Lila !　What do you mean ? "

" I'm only quoting," said Miss Howe.　And
then—" But when she isn't actually annoying me
I think I agree."

" Who said it ? " said the Baxter girl inquisitively.

" Madala.　It's the only thing I've ever heard
her say of Anita.　She never discussed Anita.　Now
of Kent she would talk by the hour.　Which proves
to me, you know, that the affair with him didn't go
very deep.　Nita quoted that description of Kent just
now, but only so far as it served her.　She carefully
forgot how it goes on.　Here, where is it ?　Ah——

He brooded like a lover over his colour-box, and as
she watched him her thoughts flew to her own small
brothers at home.　Geoff with his steam-engine, Jimmy
sorting stamps—there, there was to be found the same
ruthlessness of absorption, achieving dignity by its sheer
intensity.　She smiled over him and them.

" Keep your face still," he ordered.

She obeyed instantly, flushing; and as she did so she
thought to herself—' I could be afraid of that man,'
but a moment afterwards—' He *is* like a small boy.'

" Now that may be Kent—oh, it is Kent, of course
—but it's not Madala's attitude to Kent.　She was
not in the least afraid of him."

" Ah, but that later passage, the country passage
—that's pure Madala."

" Yes.　Just where it ceases to be Kent—' He
stoops, I suppose.　He's worn out with work.　He's
quite ordinary.'　That's not Kent."

LEGEND

" No, that's true. One doesn't know where to
have her. She muddles her trail," said Mr.
Flood.

" I call it weakness of touch not to let you know
whom she drew from," said the Baxter girl.

" Ah, but she always insisted that she didn't draw
portraits."

" Of course. They always do. If one believed
them one would never get behind the scenes, and if
one can't get behind the scenes one might as well
be mere public and read for the story," said the
Baxter girl indignantly.

" Well, you know," Miss Howe sat turning over
the pages of *The Resting-place* with careful, almost
with caressing fingers, " I don't believe she meant
to draw portraits. She had queer, old-fashioned
notions. I think she would have thought it—
treacherous."

" The portraits are there though, if you look
close enough," insisted the Baxter girl.

" Yes, but they happened in spite of her. Anyone she was fond of she took into her, in a sense :
and when her gift descended upon her and demanded
expression, then, all unconsciously, she expressed
them too. But gilded ! We find ourselves in her
books, and we never knew before how lovable we
are. You're right, Blanche, *she liked whate'er she
looked on.* And you're right too, Jasper, *Grande
amoureuse*, she was that. That capacity for loving
made her what she was. The technical facility was

152

her talent and her luck; but it was her own personality that turned it into genius."

"Then after all you admit the genius," said the Baxter girl triumphantly.

"No. No. No. My judgment says no. When I read her books in cold blood—no. But we've been talking about her. It's as if she were with us, and when she's with us my judgment goes! That's the secret of Madala Grey. She does what she likes with us. But the next generation, the people who don't know her, whether they'll find in her books what we do, is doubtful. Who wants a dried rose?"

"Yes, but Miss Serle—in the *Life?* Won't she —preserve her?"

"Preserve—exactly! But not revive. No, I'd sooner pin my faith to *The Spring Song*, although I haven't seen it. It ought to be a revelation. She eluded Nita, impishly. I've seen her do it. But there's no doubt that she gave Kent his chance."

"Every chance. She'd deny it, I suppose."

"Oh, she did." Miss Howe laughed. "Have you ever seen her in a temper? I have. I was a fool. I told her one day (you know how things come up) just something of the gossip about Kent and her. I thought it only kind. But you should have heard her. She was as healthily furious as a schoolgirl. That was so comfortable about Madala. She hadn't that terrible aloofness of really big people. She didn't withdraw into dignity. She just stormed." Miss Howe laughed again. "I

153

can see her now, raging up and down the room—
'Do you mean to say that people——? I never
heard of anything so monstrous! What has it
got to do with them? Why can't they leave
me alone? I've never done them any harm. I
wouldn't have believed it, pretending they liked
me, and letting me be friends with them, and then
saying hateful things behind my back. I'll never
speak to them again—never! That they should go
about twisting things—Why can't they mind their
own business? And dragging in Kent like that!
Oh, it does make me so wild!' 'Oh, well, my
dear,' I said to her, 'when two people see as much
of each other as you and Kent do, there's bound to
be talk.' At that she swung round on me. 'But
he's my *friend*,' she said. 'Yes,' I said, 'that's
just it.' 'But I'm not expected to marry everyone
I'm fond of!' 'Are you fond of him, Madala?'
I asked her. 'Yes,' she said directly, 'I am. I'm
awfully fond of him. I'd do anything for him,
bless his heart!' 'Well,' I said, 'you needn't be
so upset. That's all that people mean. If you're
fond of him and he—he's obviously in love with
you——' But at that she caught me up in her
quick way—'In love? Oh, you don't understand
him. Nobody understands Kent. He doesn't
understand himself. Dear old Kent!' Then she
began walking up and down the room again, but
more quietly, and talking, half to herself, as if she
had forgotten I was there, justifying herself, justi-

fying him. 'Dear old Kent! Poor old Kent! I'm awfully fond of Kent. So is he of me. But not in the right way. He's got, when he happens to think of it, a great romantic idea of the woman he wants, of the wife he wants; but the truth is, you know, that he doesn't want a wife. He wants a mother, and a sister, and a—a lover. A true lover. A patienter woman than I am. A woman who'll delight in him for his own sake, not for what he gives her. A woman who'll put him first and be content to come second with him. He'll always put his work first. He can't help it. He's an artist. Oh, not *content*. I didn't mean that. She must be too big for that—big enough to know what she misses. But a wise woman, such a loving, hungry woman. 'Half a loaf,' she'll say to herself. But she'll never have to let him hear. He's chivalrous. He'd be horrified at giving her half a loaf. He'd say—'All or nothing!' But he couldn't give her all. He couldn't spare it. So he'd give her nothing out of sheer respect for her. That's Kent. He's got his dear queer theories of life—oh, they're all right as theories—but he fits people to them, instead of them to people. Procrustes. He'd torture a woman from the kindest of motives. It's lack of imagination. Haven't you noticed?' 'Considering he's one of the great imaginative artists of the day, Madala,' I said to her, 'that's rather sweeping.' 'But that's why,' she said. 'It's just because he's

a genius. He lives on himself, in himself. Kent's
an island.' I said —' No chance of a bridge, Madala?' She shook her head. ' Not my job.' I
said I was sorry. I was, too. It would have been
so ideal, that pair. I wanted to argue it with her;
but she wouldn't listen. She said—' If I weren't
an artist too, then maybe—maybe. I'm very fond
of Kent. But no—I'd want too much. But, you
know, there's a woman somewhere, rather like me
—I hope he'll marry her. I'd love her. She'd
never be jealous of me. She'd understand. She's
me without the writing, without the outlet. She'll
pour it all into loving him. I hope she's alive somewhere. He'd be awfully happy. And if he had
children—that's what he needs. I can just see
him with children. But not my children. If I
married——' And then she flushed up to the eyes
in that way she had, as if she were fifteen. ' I—I'd
like to be married for myself, for my faults, for the
bits I don't tell anyone. Kent would hate my
faults. I'd have to hide my realest self.' She stood
staring out of the window. Then she said, still in
that rueful, childish voice—' I would like to be
liked.' ' But, my dear girl,' said I, ' what nonsense
you talk! If ever a woman had friends——' She
flung round at me again—' If I'd not written *Eden
Walls* would Anita have looked at me—or any of
you?' I said—' That's not a fair question. Your
books *are* you, the quintessence, the very best of
you.' ' But the rest of me?' she said, ' but the

156

LEGEND

rest of me?' I laughed at her. 'Well, what about the rest of you?' Then she said, in a small voice—'It feels rather out of it sometimes, Lila.'"

"I say," Mr. Flood twinkled at her, "are you going to present all this to Anita? She'd be grateful."

"Not she," said Miss Howe sharply. "Too much fact would spoil her theory. Let her spin her own web."

"Agreed. There's room for more than one biography, eh?" They laughed together a little consciously.

"You know," the blonde lady recalled them, "she must have been quite a good actress. She always seemed perfectly contented."

"Imagine Madala Grey discontented," said the Baxter girl. "How could she be?"

"Oh, Kent was at the root of that," said Miss Howe, "for all her talk."

Mr. Flood nodded.

"Yes, the lady did protest too much, if your report's correct."

"It's the only explanation and, as you said, Blanche, in her heart Anita knows it. After all, he's a somebody. Madala wouldn't be the only one who's found him attractive, eh?" She cocked an eyebrow.

"Don't be scandalous, Lila," said the blonde lady virtuously, and Mr. Flood gave his little sniff of enjoyment.

157

LEGEND

"Oh, give me five minutes," said Miss Howe cosily. "She'll be down in five minutes. I've been good all the evening. But I'm inclined to agree with her, you know, that Madala was attracted, just because Madala denied it so vehemently. Only Anita goes too far for me. She's right, of course, when she says of Kent—'Not a marrying man!' but not in the way she means it. There are dark and awful things in the history of every unmarried man, to Anita. She scents intrigue everywhere. I'm a spinster myself, but I'm not such a spidery spinster. She may be partly right. Some other man, some question-mark of a man, may have treated Madala badly. But Kent didn't. Kent isn't that sort. Intrigue would bore him. Still, he wasn't a marrying man in those days, and I think Madala was perfectly honest when she said—'Just friends.' But I think also, if you ask me, that they were far too good friends. It's not wise to be friends with a man. You must be a woman first and let him know it. I don't believe in these platonic friendships. So I think that in time Madala found out where they were making the mistake. And he didn't, or wouldn't. Oh well!" she paused expressively, "he's finding it out now. He has been all the year. Didn't you see his face when he came in tonight? Madala shouldn't have hurried. Poor Madala! Though I don't think it broke her heart, you know."

"No." The blonde lady nodded. "She was too

158

LEGEND

serene, too placid, for real passion. She could draw
it well enough, but always from the outside."

"Oh, I don't think so," said the Baxter girl.
"Think of the end of *Ploughed Fields*."

"Let's give her some credit for imagination, even
if we don't say 'genius'! I agree with Blanche.
Oh, perhaps her heart did crack just a little——"

The blonde lady struck in—

"But then Carey's a doctor. So convenient!"

"Yes," said Mr. Flood. "I always said he caught
her on the rebound."

"And then, to mix metaphors, the fat was in
the fire. Then, Kent woke up to her. Isn't it
obvious? He was fond of Madala Grey, but it
was Mrs. Carey that he fell in love with. Just like
a man!"

"Oh, I hate you," said Mr. Flood. "You
destroy my illusions. I'm like Anita. I demand
the tragic Madala."

"You can have her, I should think," said the
Baxter girl thoughtfully. "Oh, of course your
theory does seem probable as far as it goes, Miss
Howe, but——"

"But what?" said Miss Howe.

"Well, she hardly ever came to town afterwards,
did she?"

"Ah, Madala was always wise," said the blonde
lady.

Mr. Flood rubbed his hands.

"Thank-you, Beryl. We're in sympathy. And

159

it's quite a satisfying, tragical picture, isn't it?
The two artists—he with his lay figure and she with
her Hodge, and the long year between them. Can't
you see them, cheated, desirous, stretching out to
each other their impotent hands? One could make
something out of that."

"You could, Mr. Flood," said the Baxter girl
fervently.

"Out of what?" Anita was always noiseless.
I jumped to hear her voice so close behind me.

Miss Howe looked up at her quizzingly.

"Madala and—— Where *is* Kent?"

"With Mother still. He's managed her extraordinarily. She's getting sleepy, thank goodness!
He'll be down in a minute." Then, with a change
of tone—"Madala and Kent? I think not, Lila
dear."

"But you said yourself——" the Baxter girl
interposed.

"Oh no! I flung it out—a suggestion—a possi-
bility. I haven't committed myself—yet. I wish
I could be sure of Kent. He's upset my conception
of him tonight. I should have said—selfish.
Especially over Madala. But all men are selfish.
Yet, tonight——" she hesitated, playing with the
papers that lay half in, half out of the open desk.
"But who was it, if it wasn't Kent? Because
there *was* someone, you know——" And then, as
if Miss Howe's smile annoyed her beyond prudence
—"Do you think I'm inventing? Do you think

160

I've talked for amusement's sake? I tell you, she was on the verge of an elopement. *Without* benefit of clergy!"

"Anita!" Miss Howe half rose from her chair.

"We're getting it at last." Mr. Flood addressed the room. "I knew she had something up her sleeve."

"I don't believe—I won't believe it," said Miss Howe.

Then Anita smiled.

"Didn't I say she was careless about her drafts? I've a fragment here—no, I've left it in my writing-table——" and she rose as she spoke—"no name, but it's proof enough. It's an answer to some man's letter."

"But does she definitely consent——?" began the Baxter girl.

"Not in so many words. But it's obvious there was some cause or impediment, and he, whoever he is, has evidently had qualms of conscience about letting her call the world well lost for his sweet sake."

"That would rule out Kent, of course," said Miss Howe thoughtfully. "There was no reason why Kent shouldn't marry."

"We know of none," said Anita in her suggestive voice. "Isn't that as much as one can say of any man?"

"Ah!" said the Baxter girl, illuminated. I don't know why—her round eyes. I suppose, and her pursed mouth—but she reminded me of the woodcut of Minerva's owl in *Larousse*.

"So you see my prime difficulty. I've passed under review every man of her acquaintance, till I narrowed down the possible——"

"Affinities," said the blonde lady.

"—to Kent Rehan, John Carey, and this probable but unknown third. There I hang fire. Until I make up my mind on which of the three her love story hinges, I can't do more than trifle with the *Life*. And how shall I make up my mind?"

"Three?" said Mr. Flood. "Two. You can eliminate the husband. He's fifth act, not third."

"Yes, of course. But I never jump a step. Which leaves me the unknown—or Kent."

The blonde lady leant forward rather eagerly—

"Nita! Where's that letter?"

"I'll get it." She went across the room to her writing-table.

The Baxter girl twisted her head.

"I say! He's coming down the stairs."

"If she read aloud that draft——" the blonde lady's drawl had disappeared. She glittered like an excited schoolgirl—"he might recognize——"

"You mean——?" Mr. Flood raised his eyebrows but Anita, fumbling with her keys, did not hear.

"It would be nice to be sure," said the blonde lady.

"It's rather cruel, isn't it?" said Miss Howe uneasily.

LEGEND

" Why ? It'll be printed in the *Life*. Besides, it may not have been written to him."

" That's why," said Miss Howe.

" It would be nice to be *quite* sure," said the blonde lady again. And as she spoke Kent Rehan came into the room.

At once I got up, with some blind, blundering idea, I believe, of stopping him, of frustrating them, but Anita was nearer to him than I.

" Is she asleep ? Very good of you, Kent. Sit here, Kent. Jenny, is the window open in the passage ? Very cold. I never knew such a draught."

I went out to see. I had to do as I was told. Besides, how could I have stopped them or him ? Yet I was shaking with anger and disgust at them, and at myself for my hateful tongue-tied youth and insignificance. An older woman would have known what to do. Shaking with cold too—Anita was right—it was bitter cold in the passage. I could hardly see my way to the window for the fog. It was open an inch at the bottom, and at my touch it rattled down with a bang that echoed oddly. For an instant I thought it was a knock at the hall door. I stood a minute, quite startled, peering down into the black well of the hall. But there was no second knock, only the fog-laden draught of the passage came rushing up at me again, and again Anita called to me to come in and shut the door. I did so : and because it rattled, wedged

163

it with the screw of paper that lay near it on the
floor, the crumpled telegram that Kent Rehan had
dropped when he first came in. Then, still shivering
a little, I sat down where I was. I didn't want to
go nearer. I knew my face was tell-tale. I didn't
want to have the Baxter girl looking at me, and
maybe saying something. I could hear them in the
other room well enough. Anita's voice seemed to
cut through the thick air. There was a letter in
her hand. She was twisting it about as if she
couldn't find the first page.

" —obviously a draft." She held it away from
her. Anita was long-sighted.

" Dear—dear——

Then it breaks off and begins again. You see? "
She displayed it to them.

" Dearest——"

" Why, how clearly it's written ! " The Baxter
girl peered at it. " That's quite a beautiful hand.
That's not Madala's scrawl."

The blonde lady looked at them through half
shut lids.

" Ah ! It's been written slowly——"

" As if she loved writing it ! " The Baxter girl
flushed. " Did *she* know about that sort of thing
—that sentimental sort of thing ? I should have
thought her too—oh, too splendid, removed—you
know what I mean."

164

LEGEND

"I don't suppose she talked about it," said Anita coldly. "She was not of your generation." And then, to the others—"I assure you, this letter shook me. Even I never dreamed of this side of her. Listen." She read aloud in her measured voice—

"Dearest—

I wanted your letter so. I reckoned out the posts, and the distances, and your busyness. I thought that in two days you would probably write, and then I gave you another day's grace because you hate writing letters, and because I thought you couldn't dream how much I missed you—how much, how *soon*, I wanted to hear. And then to get your letter the very next day, before I could begin to look for it (but I did look !). Why, you must have written as soon as the train was out of the station ! You missed me just as much then ?

But it's a mad letter, you know. It makes me laugh and cry. It's so sensible—and so silly. 'Fame', 'career', 'reputation', 'position'—why do you fling these words at me ? *I* am making a sacrifice ? Darling, haven't you eyes ? Don't you understand that you're my world ? All these other things, since I've known you, they're shadows, they're toys, I don't want them. The reviews of my new book—I've never been so delighted at getting any—but why ? D'you know why ? To show them to you—to watch you shake with laughter as you read them. When a flattering letter turns up, I save it to show you as if it were gold, because I think— 'Perhaps it'll make him think more of me.' Isn't it idiotic ? But I do. And all the while I glory in the knowledge that all these things, all the fuss and fame,

165

LEGEND

don't mean a brass button to you—or to me, my dear,
or to me.

And yet you write me a solemn letter about ' making
a sacrifice,' ' abdicating a position.'

Don't be—humble   And yet I like you in this mood.
Because it won't last !   I won't *let* it.   It's I who am
not good enough.   If you knew how I tip-toe sometimes.   You're so much bigger than I am.   I lie in
bed at nights, and all the things I've done wrong in
my life, all the twisty, tortuous, feminine things, all
the lies and cowardices and conceits, come and sting
me.   I'm so bitterly ashamed of them.   I feel I've got
to tell you about them all, and yet that if I do you'll
turn me out of your heart.   If you did that—if you
were disappointed—if you got tired of me—it turns me
sick with fear.

I'm a fool to tear myself.   I know you love me.
And when you're with me I forget all that.   I'm just
happy.   When you're there it's like being in the blazing
sunshine.   Can ' celebrity ' give me that sunshine ?
Can ' literature ' fill my emptiness ?   Are the books I
write children to love me with your eyes ?   Oh, you
fool !

Oh, of course, I know you don't mean it.   It's just
that you think you ought to protest.   But suppose I
took you at your word ?   Suppose I said that, on careful
consideration, I felt that I wanted to lead my own life
instead of yours ?   that—how does the list run ?—my
Work, my Circle of Friends, my Career, were too much
to give up for—you ?   What would you say—no, do ?
for even I, (and the sun's in my eyes) even I can't call
you eloquent !   But what would you do if I wouldn't
come to you ?

Oh, my darling, my darling, you needn't be afraid.
I'd rather be a door-keeper in the house of my God——

I'm changed   What have you done to me ?   Other

166

people notice it. My friends are grown critical of me.
Only yesterday someone (no-one you know) sneered at
me—'In love? Oh well, you'll get over it. It's a
phase.' You know, they don't understand. I'm not
' in love ', but I love you. There's the difference. I
love you. I shall love you till I die. Till——? As if
death could blot you out for me! I used to believe
in death. I used to believe it ended everything. But
now, since I've known you, I can never die You've
poured into me an immortal spirit——"

" Go on," breathed the Baxter girl.

" It breaks off there. It's not signed. It was
never sent."

" She had that much wisdom, then." The
blonde lady's laughter came to us over Mr. Flood's
shoulder. " That's not the letter to send to any
man. Giving herself away—giving us all away——"

" To any man? To what man? There's the
point. You see the importance. It's the heart of
the secret. Who is it? For whom was she ready
to give up, in her own words, name, friends,
career——? "

" Well, practically she did that, didn't she, when
she married Carey? She buried herself in the
country. . She didn't write a line. You said yourself that she put her career behind her. Why
shouldn't it be written to Carey? "

" Oh, don't be absurd. It's Carey that makes
it impossible. How could Carey have written a
letter needing such an answer? Little he cared.
What was her genius to him? Isn't it obvious,

isn't it plain as print, that Carey happened, Carey
and all he stands for, *after* the writing of this letter,
because of some hitch? Why wasn't the letter
sent? What happened? What folly? What mis-
understanding? What disillusionmént? What
realization of danger?—to send her, with that letter
half written, into Carey's arms? Carey, that stick,
that ordinary man! And on the top of it *The
Resting-place* comes out, the *cri du cœur*—or, if
you like, Lila, the satire—(for I'm beginning to
believe you're right) the satire of *The Resting-place*.
I tell you, I smell tragedy."

"It's supposition, it's mere supposition," said
Miss Howe impatiently.

"Isn't all detective work supposition to begin
with? Wait till I've made my book. Wait till
I've sifted my evidence, till I've ranged it, stick
and brick, step by step, up, up, up, to the letter."

Suddenly from where he sat, half way between
me and them, Kent spoke—

"Anita, you can't publish that letter."

Her face, all their faces, turned towards us. She
stared.

"Why not?" And then—"Why do you sit
out there? Come here. Come into the light."

He did not stir.

She frowned, puckering her eyes.

"Such a fog," she said fretfully. "I can't see
you. Can't you keep that door shut, Jenny?"
Then—"Well, Kent—why not? Why not?"

LEGEND

He said slowly—

" It's not decent."

She flared at once.

" Decent ! Not decent ! What on earth do you mean ? "

He kept her waiting while he thought it out.

" I mean—it's not right, it's not fair. To whomever it was written, that's her business, not our business. And that letter—— It's vile, anyway, publishing her letters."

She stared at him in a sort of angry bewilderment.

" But why ? I shall write her life. One always does print letters."

" Not that sort of letter," he said.

" But don't you see," she cried, " that *that* letter, just *that* letter——"

He said—

" That's why. How dare you read that letter here—aloud—tonight ? It—it's ghoulish."

" Kent ! " There was outrage in her voice.

" But Kent——" Miss Howe intervened—" we knew her—we care—it's in all reverence——"

And Mr. Flood—

" My dear man, she's not a private character. The lives that will be written ! Anita's may be the classic, but it won't be the only one. Letters are bound to be printed—every scrap she ever wrote. Nobody can stop it. It's only a question of time. The public has its rights."

" To what ? " He turned savagely. " You've

had her books. She's given enough. Will you
leave her nothing private, nothing sacred?"

"But Kent, can't you see——" Anita had an
air of pushing Miss Howe and Mr. Flood from her
road—"aren't you artist enough to see——? A
writer, a woman like Madala, she has no private
life. She lives to write. She lives what she writes.
She *is* what she writes. She gives her soul to the
world. She leaves her riddle to be read. Don't
you see? to be read. That's what I'm doing.
That's what I'm going to do—read her—for the
rest of you, for the public. Because—because they
care, because we all care. It's done in all honour.
It's a tribute. And for what I am going to do, such
a letter is the key."

She spoke softly, sweetly, persuasively. She
wooed him to agree with her. She was extraordinarily eager for his approval. And the approval
of the others she did win. They were all murmuring
agreement.

His eyes strayed over them, undecidedly, seeking
—not help. I do not know what he sought, but
his eyes found mine.

"*You*——" he said to me—"would you want
your letter——?"

Anita's voice thrust in sharply. In the instant
the pleading, the beauty, the woman, was gone
from it. It was cold and shrill.

"Jenny's views can hardly concern us."

But he did not listen to her. He had drawn

some answer from me that satisfied him. He got up.

" Oh," I cried beneath my breath, and I think I touched his arm—" you won't let her? "

He shook his head. Then he went across to where Anita stood, her eyes on him, on me, while she listened to Miss Howe whispering at her shoulder.

" Look here, Anita ! " he began.

" I'm looking," she said.

He checked a moment, puzzled. Then he went on—

" That letter—you can't print it. You've no right. It's not your property."

She waved it aside.

" I shall be literary executor. She promised. It's mine if it's anyone's. It's no good, Kent, it goes into the book. Nothing can alter that. Nothing——"

Then she stopped dead. There was that same odd look in her eye as there had been when she watched us—that flicker of curiosity, and behind it the same gleam of inexplicable anger.

" Look here——" she said very deliberately— " look *you* here—what has it got to do with you ? "

It was not the words, it was the tone. It was shameless. It was as if she had cried aloud her hateful questions—' Did you love her ? ' ' What was there between you ? ' ' I want to know it all.

171

it tears me not to know.' But what she said to him, and before he could answer, was—

"If, of course—anyone—had any right—could prove any right——" She broke off, watching him closely. But he said nothing. "If," she said, and poked with her finger, "if that letter—if you recognized it—if that were the rough draft of a letter that had been sent——"

He stared down at her. His face was bleak.

"You'll get no copy from me, Anita!"

"Oh!" She caught her breath, fierce and wicked as a cat with a bird, yet shrinking as a cat does, supple, ears flat. "I only meant—I said *right*. If anyone—if you could satisfy me—if you have any right——"

He said—

"I have no right."

"Oh well, then!" She shrugged her shoulders.

"But," he held stubbornly to his purpose, "whoever has a right to it—you can't print that letter."

She laughed at him.

"You'll see! You'll see!"

"Yes," he said, "I'll see."

They held each other's eyes, angry, angry. I felt how Kent Rehan loathed her. And she—yes, she must have hated him. She was all bitterness and triumph and defiance. Yet all the time I was wanting to catch him by the arm and say—'Be kind to her. Say something kind and she'll give

172

in.' I knew it. He had only to say in that instant
—'Anita, I beg of you——' and she would have
given him the letter. I knew it. I know it. I
don't know how I knew it, but I was sure. But he
was a man: of course he saw nothing. He was
very angry. He looked big and fine. I wondered
that she could stand outfacing him.

But she, for answer, picked up the letter, and
affected to search through it.

"Had I finished? Where was I? Ah, yes—
'An immortal spirit——'"

His hand came down heavily and swept the light
table aside.

"You can't do it. You shan't do it. By God
you shan't."

How it happened I couldn't see. He was too
quick. But at one moment she held the letter, and
in the next he had it, and was kneeling at the
grate, while she cried out—

"Kent!" And then—"Lila! Jasper! Stop
him!"

Nobody could have stopped him. There was no
flame, but the fire still burned, a caked red and
black lump, smouldering on cinders. He picked it
up—with his naked hands—thrust in the crumpled
stiff paper, and smashed it down again, so that the
lump split, and still held it pressed down, with
naked hands, till the sheet had charred and shrivelled
into nothing. I suppose it all happened in a few
seconds, but it seemed like hours. I was in a train

M

smash once : I wasn't hurt; but I remember that I
came out of it with just the same sense of being
battered and aged.   This scene I had only watched :
I had not shared in it : I was still in the little outer
room. Yet I was shaken. I heard Mr. Flood call
out—"Kent, you crazy fool!" I heard Anita—
"Let me go, Lila!" And then the women were
between me and him, and I could only see their
backs, and there was a babel of voices, and I found
myself sitting like a fool, clutching at the arms of
my chair, and saying over and over again—"Oh,
his hands, his hands, his poor hands!" The tears
were running down my cheeks.

But nobody noticed me. They were all too busy.
The group had shifted a little. The Baxter girl
was edged out of it, and I watched her for a moment
as she sat down again, her cheeks flaming, her eyes
as bright as wet pebbles. She looked—it's the
only word—consumptive with excitement. Every
now and then she tried not to cough. I heard
her saying—"It's the fog, it's the awful fog!"
defensively. But nobody listened. They were all
watching Anita.

Anita was dreadful. She was tremulous with
anger. She was like a pendulum with the check
taken away. Her whole body shook. She couldn't
finish her sentences. She talked to everyone at
once.

Miss Howe had her by the arm   Miss Howe was
trying to quiet her—

"My dear woman—steady now! You don't want a row, you know! You've got the rest of the papers." But she might have talked to the wind.

"He comes into my house—my property—in my own house—— It's an outrage! Kent, it's an outrage!"

Kent Rehan rose to his feet. It was like a rock breaking through that froth of women. He stood a moment, nervously, brushing the black from his hands and wincing as he did so. Then he looked up. His eyes met hers. He flushed.

"Kent! Kent!" She flung off Miss Howe.

The intensity of reproach in her voice startled me, and I think it startled him. I found myself thinking —'All this anger for what? for a burnt paper? It's impossible! But then—then what's the matter with her?'

He said awkwardly—

"I'm sorry, Anita."

"*You!*" she cried panting—"*You*, to interfere! D'you know what you've done, what you've tried to do? Will you take everything, you and he? Haven't I my work too? Oh, what you've had from her, what you've had from her! And now you cheat me!"

He was bewildered. He said again—

"I'm sorry, Anita."

She came close to him. Her little hands were clenched. There was a wail in her voice—

"You! Aren't you friends with me? Didn't I

175

share her with you ? Isn't she my work too ? What would you say if I came to your house and saw your work, your life work that she'd made possible, your pictures that are her, all her—and slashed them with a knife ? What would you do if I'd done that, if I'd cut it to ribbons, your *Spring Song ?* "

That moved him. I saw a sort of comprehension lighting his stubborn face. The artist in her touched the artist in him. Of what lay behind the artist he had no knowledge. But he said, quite humbly—

" Anita, I'm sorry ! "

Yet I knew that he was not sorry for what he had done.

" Sorry ! Sorry ! Much good your sorrow does ! " she shrilled, and I saw him stiffen again. She was strange. She valued him, that was so plain, and yet, it almost seemed in self-defence, she was always at her worst with him. " Sorry ! It was the key of the book. You've spoilt my book."

" Nita ! Nita ! One letter ! " Miss Howe was almost comical in her dislike of the scene. " As if you couldn't pull it off without that." She pulled her aside, lowering her voice—" Nita, what's the use of a row ? Pull yourself together. Put yourself in his place. Besides—you can't afford——" She looked at Kent significantly. Anita's pale glance followed her and so their eyes met again. She was angry and sullen and irresolute. Another woman would have been near tears.

" Kent," she began. And then—" Kent—if we

176

quarrel——We're too old to quarrel——If you had a shadow of excuse——"

He waited.

She took fire again because he did not meet her half way.

" But if you think you've stopped me——" she cried. She broke off with a laugh and a new idea— " As if," she said slowly and scornfully, " as if Madala would have cared ! "

He said distinctly—

" You didn't know her. You'd never understand——"

" Ah," she said, pressing forward to him, " why do you take that tone? What is it I don't understand? If you'd help me with what you know, it could be big stuff. I'd forgive you for the letter if you'd work with me." She hung on his answer.

But he only said, not looking at her, in the same tone—

" You'd never understand." And then, with an effort—" I'll go, Anita. I'm going. I'd better go."

Without waiting for her answer he went across the room to the little sofa near me where the hats and coats lay piled. I heard him fumbling for his things.

But Anita went back to the others. The watching group seemed to open to receive, to enclose her. Her head had touched the lamp as she passed under it, and set it swaying wildly, so that I could scarcely see their faces in that shift of light and shadow

177

LEGEND

through the thickened air. But I heard her angry
laugh, and her voice overtopping the murmur—
"Mad! He was always mad! If he weren't such
an old friend——" And then the Baxter girl's
voice—"Think of the sketches there must be!"
And Miss Howe—"What I say is—you don't want
to quarrel!" And hers again—"Did you hear
him? *I* not understand Madala! Mad, I tell you!
If I don't know Madala——"

It was at that moment that I looked up and saw a
woman standing in the doorway.

"Anita!" I murmured warningly. But my
voice did not reach her, and indeed, she and the
little gesticulating group in the further room seemed
suddenly far away. The air had been thickening for
the last hour, and now, with the opening of the door,
the fog itself came billowing in on either side of the
newcomer as water streams past a ship. It flooded
the room, soundlessly, almost, I remember thinking,
purposefully, as if it would have islanded us, Kent
and me. It affected me curiously. I felt muffled.
I knew I ought to get up and call again to Anita
or attend to the visitor myself, but the quiet seemed
to dull my wits. I found myself placidly wondering
who she was and why she did not come in; but I
made no movement to welcome her. I just sat still
and stared.

She was a tall girl—woman—for either word
fitted her: she had brown hair. She was dressed
in—I should have said, if you had asked me, that

178

LEGEND

I could remember every detail, and I can in my own mind; but when I try to write it down, it blurs. But I know that there was blue in her dress, and bright colours. It must have been some flowered stuff. She looked—it's a silly phrase—but she looked like a spring day. I wanted her to come into the room and drive away the fog that was making me blink and feel dizzy. There was a gold ring on her finger: yes, and her hands were beautiful—strong, white hands. In one she held the brass candle-stick that stood in the hall, and with the other she sheltered the weak flame from the draught. Yet not only with her hand. Her arm was crooked maternally, her shoulder thrust forward, her hip raised, in a gesture magnificently protecting, as though the new-lit tallow-end were fire from heaven. Her whole body seemed sacredly involved in an act of guardianship. But half the glory of her pose—and it was lovely enough to make me catch my breath—was its unconsciousness; for her attention was all ours. Her eyes, as she listened to the group by the hearth, were sparkling with amusement and that tolerant, deep affection that one keeps for certain dearest, foolish friends. It was evident that she knew them well.

"Can't you keep that door shut, Jenny? The draught——"

Anita's back was towards me. Her voice, as she spoke over her shoulder, rang high, muffled, injurious, and—I laughed. In a flash the stranger's eyes were

179

on me, and I found myself thrilling where I sat, absurdly startled for the moment, because—she knew me too! She knew me quite well. She was smiling at me, not vaguely as who should say—'Oh, surely I've seen you somewhere?' but with intimate, disturbing knowledge. It was the glance that a doctor gives you, the swift, acquainted glance that, without offence, deciphers you. I was not offended either, only curious and—attracted. She looked so friendly. I half began to say—' But when? but where?' but her bearing overruled me. Her mouth was pursed conspiratorially : if her hand had been free she would have put a finger to her lip. I smiled back at her, flattered to be partner in her un-comprehended secret. But I was curious—oh, I was curious! It was incredible to me that Anita and the rest should stand, subduing their voices to the soft, thick stillness that she and the fog between them had brought into the room, and yet remain uncon-scious of her vivid presence. I was longing to see their faces when they should at last turn and see her, and yet, if you understand, I was afraid lest they should turn too soon and break the pleasant numb-ness that was upon me. And upon them—the spell was upon them too. It was the look in her eyes, not glamorous, but kind. It healed. It passed like a drowse across the squabblers at the table : it stilled Anita's feverish monologue. Indeed the room had grown very still. There was no sound left in it but the slurring of the lamp. It rested upon Kent as he stood in dumb misery. and I watched the strained lines of his body slacken and grow easier beneath it. At that—at that ease she gave him—suddenly I loved her.

And as if I had spoken, as if I had touched her with my hand, her eyes, that had grown heavy with his trouble, turned, brightening, upon me, as if I were the answer to a problem, the lifting of a care. But what the problem was I could not then tell; for, staring as she made me—as she made me—into her divining eyes, I saw in them not her thought but my own at last made clear to me—my dream, my hope, my will and my desire, new-born and naked, and, I swear it, bodiless to me before that night and that hour. It was too soon. I was not ready. It shamed me and I flinched, my glance wandering helplessly away like a dog's when you have forced it to look at you. And so noticed, idly, uncomprehending at first, and then with a stiffening of my whole body, that her hand did not show as other hands, blood-red against the light she screened, but coldly luminous, like the fingers of a cloud through which the moon is shining : and that her breast was motionless, unstirred by any breath.

Then I was afraid.

I felt my skin rising. I felt my bones grow cold. I could not move. I could not breathe. I could not think.

A voice came out of the fog that had thickened to

LEGEND

a wall between the rooms—a voice, thin, remote,
like a trunk call—

"*Can't* you keep that door shut, Jenny? The
draught——" and was cut off again by the sudden
crash of an overturned chair. There was a rush and
a cry—a madman's voice, shouting, screaming,
groaning—

"Madala Grey! My God, Madala Grey!" and
Kent's huge body, hurling against the door, pitched
and fell heavily.

For the door was shut.

I ran to him. He was shaken and half stunned,
but he struggled to his feet. It was dreadful to see
him. He was like a frightened horse, shivering and
sweating. His lips were loose and he muttered
unevenly as if the words came without his will. I
caught them as I helped him; the same words—
always the same words.

I got him to the sofa while the rest of them crowded
and clamoured, and then I found myself taking com-
mand. I made them keep off. I sent Anita for
water and a towel and I bathed his forehead where
he had cut it on the moulding of the door. Mr.
Flood wanted to send for a doctor, but I wouldn't
have it. I knew how he would hate it. Then
someone—the Baxter girl, I think—giggled hysteric-
ally and said something about a black eye tomorrow,
and then—"How did it happen?" "Did you see,
Miss Summer?" And at that they all began to
clamour again like an orchestra after a solo, repeating

182

ᵢ all their voices—" Yes, what happened? What ᴏn earth was it? Did you see him? Some sort of a seizure? I told you twice to shut that door. The draught—— Are you better now, old man? Kent —what happened?"

They were crowding round him again. He pointed a shaking finger.

" She saw," he said. " She knows——"

" Jenny?" Anita turned on me sharply, an employer addressing a servant at fault. " Oh, of course—you were in here too. What happened then?"

I had a helpless moment.

" Well?" she demanded.

I stared at her. It was incredible, but there was actually jealousy in her voice. It said, pitifully plainly—'Again I have missed the centre of a situation!'

" Well?" she repeated. And then—" If you saw something——" She altered the phrase—" Tell us what you saw."

But I had not missed the quick fear that had shown, for a moment, in Kent's eyes—fear of betrayal even while his tongue was betraying him.

I laughed. I thought to myself as I answered, ' Oh, I am doing this beautifully!' And I was. My voice sounded perfectly natural, not a bit high. I had plenty of words. I said, most jauntily—

" Oh, Cousin Nita, I could hardly see my own nose. The fog had been simply pouring in. My fault—I didn't latch the door properly, I suppose. And then you called. and Mr. Rehan went to shut it for me, and he slithered on the mat, and——"

" I see ! "

" Of course ! Parquet——" The Baxter girl took a step or two and pirouetted back to us. " Perfect ! You ought to give a dance, Miss Serle."

Anita made no answer, but taking the can and the towel she opened the door of dispute, and, stooping an instant on the threshold to lift some small object from the floor, went out of the room. We heard her set down her load on the landing, and the rattle of the sash as she threw up the window, paused, and shut it again. She came back. A fresh inflow of acrid vapour preceded her and set us coughing. It was the stooping, I suppose, that had reddened her cheeks, for she was flushed when she came back to us. It was the only time that I ever saw my cousin with a colour. She spoke to us, a little gaspingly, as if the fog had caught her too by the throat—

" Jenny's quite right. One can't see an inch in front of one. No—not a cab in hearing. You'll have to resign yourselves to staying on indefinitely. What ? oh, what nonsense, Kent ! As if I'd let you go in that state ! Besides, there's Jasper's poem. Are you going away without hearing it ? " The soft monologue continued as she shepherded them to the fire. " That's always the way—one talks—one gets no work done. Get under the light, Jasper ! Beryl, help me to move the table. Oh yes, Jasper, I forgot to tell you, I met Roy Huth the other day and he had just read——"

I heard a movement behind me. I turned. Kent had half risen. He spoke—

" Sit down. Sit down here." He touched the cushion beside him.

I shook my head.

" Not yet. My cousin——"

" Ah——"

We were silent.

I watched Anita. She stood a few moments in unsmiling superintendence, while the women settled themselves and Mr. Flood sorted his papers and cleared his throat. Then, as I had known she would do, she returned soft-footed to her purpose. At the same moment I left Kent Rehan's side. When she reached the archway between the two rooms, I was there.

" And now——" she confronted me—" what happened ? "

" I told you."

She smiled.

" Did you ? I have forgotten. Tell me again."

" Anita—he slipped. He fell. He was shutting the door."

" Did he replace this ? " She opened her little hand. The wedge of paper that I had twisted lay on her palm. " It was shut in the door when I opened it just now." She waited a moment. Then, with a certain triumph—" Well ? "

185

I said nothing. What was there to say?
She tossed it from her.

"Don't be silly, Jenny! What was it? *Who*
was it?" Her eyes were horribly intelligent.

"He slipped. He fell. He was shutting the
door." I felt I could go on saying that for ever and
ever.

The red patches in her cheeks deepened. She
spoke past me, rudely, furiously—

"I intend to know. I've a perfect right——
Kent, I intend to know."

I put out my arms carelessly, though my heart
was thudding, and rested them against the door-
posts.

"He's shaken—a heavy man like that. Better
leave him alone."

"I intend to know," she insisted. And then—
"Jenny! *Jenny!* Let me pass."

"No!" I said.

For a second we stood opposed, and in that second
I realized literally for the first time (so dominating
had her personality been) that she was shorter than
I. She was dwindling before my eyes. I found myself looking down at her with almost brutal com-
posure. That I had ever been afraid of her was the
marvel! For I was young, and she was elderly. I
was strong, and she was weak. Her bare arms were
like sticks, but mine were round and supple, and I
could feel the blood tingle in them as my grip tightened on the wood-work. She was only Anita Serle,

the well-known writer; but I was Jenny Summer, and Kent was needing me.

"Jenny—you will be sorry!" Her eyes and her voice were one threat. Such eyes! Eyes whose pupils had dilated till the irids were mere threads that encircled jealousy itself—jealousy black and bitter—jealousy that had stolen upon us as the fog had done, obscuring, soiling, stifling friend and enemy alike—jealousy of a gift and a great name, of a dead woman and a living man and their year of happiness —jealousy beyond reason, beyond pity—jealousy insatiable, already seeking out fresh food, turning deliberately, vengefully, upon Kent and upon me.

I felt sick. I had never dreamed that there could be such feelings in the world. And now she was going to Kent, to probe and lacerate and poison—

"No!" I said.

Actually she believed that she could pass me!

I still held fast by the door-posts, and she did not use her hands. We were silent and decorous, but for an instant our bodies fought. She was pressed against me, panting—

"*No!*" I said.

Then she fell away, and without another word turned and went back into the other room.

I saw Miss Howe whisper some question. There was an instant's silence. Then her answer came—

"Much better leave him alone. Yes—rather shaken—a heavy man like that."

187

LEGEND

It was defeat. She was using my very words, because, for all her fluency, she had none with which to cover it.

I was sorry. I felt a brute. But what else could I have done? I stood a moment watching her recover herself. Then I went back to Kent.

He did not look up, but he moved a little to give me room. I sat down beside him. We were shut away between the wall and the window, in the shadow, out of sight of the others. It was very peaceful. Now and then I looked at Kent, but he was staring before him. He had forgotten all about me again, I knew. But I was content. It made me happy to be sitting by him. My thoughts hopped about like birds after crumbs. I remember wondering what I should do on the morrow—where I should go? That Anita would have me in the house another twenty-four hours was not likely. I had ten pounds. I did not care. I knew that I ought to be anxious, but I could not realize the need. I could not think of anything but him; yet I was afraid to speak to him. He sat so still. His face was set in schooled and heavy lines. There came a stir and a clash of voices from the other room, but he did not seem to hear it. It was only the end of a poem. In a little it had settled down again into the same monotonous hum, but for a moment I had thought that it was the break-up, and after that I had no peace. It had scared me. It made me realize that I had only a few minutes—half an hour at most—and that then he

would be going away—and when should I see him
again? Never—maybe never! He had his life
all arranged. He didn't even know my name. I
felt desperate. I couldn't let him go. I didn't
know what to do. I only knew that—that I couldn't
bear it if he went away from me.

It was then that he moved and straightened himself in his chair with a sigh, that heavy, long-drawn
sigh that men give when they make an end. ' Work
or play, joy or grief, it's done with. And now——? '
Such a sigh as you never hear from women. But
then we are not wise at ending things.

I thought that he was getting up, that he was
going then and there, and instinctively I hurried
into speech, daring anything—everything—his own
thoughts of me—rather than let him go.

" Yes—that's over ! " I translated softly.

He turned with such a stare that I could have
smiled.

" I meant that. How did you know ? "

" Why shouldn't I know ? " I did smile then. It
made him smile back at me, but doubtfully, unwil-
lingly.

" Can you read thoughts—too ? " The last word
seemed to come out in spite of himself.

" Not always. Yours I can." My face was burn-
ing. But I could have spared myself the shame that
made it burn, for he did not understand. My voice
said nothing to him. My face showed him nothing.
He was thinking about himself. But he leant for-

ward in that way he has—a dear way—of liking to talk to you.

"Can you? I never can. Only when I paint. I can put them into paint, of course. But not words. *She* said——" and all through the subsequent talk he avoided the name—" she said it was laziness, a lazy mind. But I always told her that that was her fault. I—we—her people—were just wool: she knitted us into our patterns. She was a wonder. You know, she—she was good for one. She was like bread—bread and wine——" His voice strained and flagged.

I nodded.

"Yes. I felt that too."

He glanced sideways at me.

"Ah, then you knew her?" His voice (or I imagined it) had chilled. It began to say, that faint chill, that if I too were of ' the set,' he could not be at ease. But I would not give him time to think awry.

"No, no! Only tonight. But I do know her."

" Tonight ? "

" Tonight," I said and looked at him.

" Then——" his hand tightened on the chair, " you saw? I was right? You *did* see? "

" I saw—something," I admitted.

" Some-one ? "

I nodded.

His face lighted up. He pulled in his chair to me.

" Her hands—did you notice her hands? I have

190

a drawing of them somewhere. I'll show it to you——" He stopped short: Then—"What is your name?" he asked me.

"Jenny. Jenny Summer."

He considered that fact for a moment and put it aside again.

"I'd like you to see it. Anita will want it for that damned scrap-book of hers. She'll be worrying at me—they all will."

"You won't let it go?" I said quickly.

He shook his head.

"No. But they can't understand why. They can't understand anything. They thought I was mad just now. So I was, for that matter. To see her again, you know—to see her again——"

"I know," I said.

He laughed nervously.

"Hallucination, of course. Thought transference. What you please. They'd say so. Do you think so? And I'd been thinking of my picture of her. Oh, I admit it. So we must look at the matter in the light of common-sense."

"But I saw her too."

His eyes softened, and his voice.

"Yes. You were there. That's comfort. You saw her too—standing there with her dear hands full of cowslips——"

"A torch," I said.

"Cowslips——" he checked on the word. "*What?*"

"She was carrying a candle," I insisted. "It had just been lighted. She was holding it so carefully."

We stared at each other.

"You're sure?"

"Sure."

He fell back wearily in his chair.

"What's the good of talking? She's dead. That's the end of it. I was dreaming. Of course. But when you said that you saw, for a moment I believed—— What does it matter? What does it matter anyway? But her hands were full of cowslips."

I turned to him eagerly. I knew what to say. It was as if the words were being whispered to me.

"That was your Madala Grey. But mine—how could she be the same? Oh, can't you see? We've never seen the real Madala Grey. She gave—she became—to each of us—what we wanted most. She wrote down our dreams. She *was* our dreams. Can't you see what she meant to my cousin? Anita toils and slaves for her little bit of greatness. But *she* was born royal. That's why Anita hates her so—hates her and worships her. Why, she's been a sort of star to you all—a symbol—a legend—

But the real Madala Gray—she wasn't like that. She was just a girl. She was hungry all the time. She was wanting her human life. And he, the man they laugh at, 'the thing she married,' he did love that real Madala Grey. Why, he didn't even know

192

of the legend. Don't you see that that was what
she wanted? She could take from him as well as
give. Life—the bread and wine—they shared it.
Oh, and it's him I pity now, not you. Not you,"
I said again, while my heart ached over him. "You
—can't you see what she showed you? Not herself——"

"What then?" he said harshly.

I made the supreme effort.

"But what -a woman—one day—would be to
you."

I thought the silence would never break.

The strange courage that had been in me was
suddenly gone. I felt weak and friendless. I
wanted to cry. I waited and waited till I could
bear it no longer. Then I lifted my eyes desperately,
with little hope, to read in his face what the end
should be.

I found him looking at me fixedly—*at* me, you
understand, not through me to a subject that
absorbed him, but at me myself. It was as if he
were seeing me for the first time. No—as if he
recognized me at last.

Then the doubts went, and the shame and the
loneliness. It made me so utterly happy, that look
on his face. I felt my heart beating fast.

He said then, slowly—I can remember the words,
the tone and pitch of his voice, the very shaping of his
mouth as he said it—

"Do you know—it's strange—you remind me of

LEGEND

her. You are very like her. You are very like Madala Grey."

The hunger in his voice hurt me. I wanted to put my arms round him and comfort him. I might have done it, for I knew I was still but half real to him. But I sat still—only, with such a sense in my heart of a trust laid upon me, of an inheritance, of a widening and golden future, I said to him—

"Yes. I know."

October 1917—*April* 1919

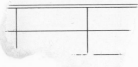

DATE DUE